THE RIDDLE OF THE SEA

THE RIDDLE OF THE SEA

JONNE ✳ KRAMER

TRANSLATED BY LAURA WATKINSON

Piccadilly
PRESS

Original Dutch language edition, *Het raadsel van de zee*, first published by
BILLY BONES, an imprint of MEIS & MAAS, Amsterdam, in 2019

This publication has been made possible with financial support from
the Dutch Foundation for Literature.

N ederlands
letterenfonds
dutch foundation
for literature

First published in Great Britain in 2022 by
PICCADILLY PRESS
4th Floor, Victoria House, Bloomsbury Square, London WC1B 4DA
Owned by Bonnier Books, Sveavägen 56, Stockholm, Sweden
www.piccadillypress.co.uk

A CIP catalogue record for this book is available from the British Library.

ISBN: 978-1-80078-037-8
Also available as an ebook and in audio

1

Printed and bound by Clays Ltd, Elcograf S.p.A.

Piccadilly Press is an imprint of Bonnier Books UK
www.bonnierbooks.co.uk

For Papa

1

THE HARBOUR OF ROTTENHERRING

How long does a seagull live? It's a question Ravian has often asked himself. His dad would be sure to know. He always has an answer for every question. As Ravian washes the dirty glasses, he wonders how old his friend Marvin the seagull is. He must be at least eight by now, because Ravian found him on the beach eight years ago, when he was four. It's a shame Marvin can't tell him. When his dad's back, he'll ask him.

Ravian puts the clean beer glasses in the cupboard. You can't stack more than three or they fall over. The boring work makes his thoughts wander. He plays a game, asking himself funny questions. How many tentacles does a jellyfish have? How old is the sea? How many seahorses would it take to pull a ship? He doesn't know the answer to any of them.

As always, the pub is busy. It's the only place to have a drink in the harbour village of Rottenherring. There are sailors sitting at all the tables – which are actually old barrels – and they're all talking away. There are oil lamps on the walls, giving off a cosy orange glow.

'Hey! Freckleface! Fill one of those beer glasses with rum for me!' shouts Captain Agnar, who is sitting in his usual place at the bar, wearing his large hat.

'A beer glass? That's far too big!' says Ravian.

The boss, with her strong arms, grabs the glass from Ravian's hands and puts it in the cupboard. She's blonde and a bit chubby, with round, red cheeks. And she always wears the same dirty apron.

'Don't be so daft, Agnar,' she says to the man, pouring a smaller glass for him.

He looks sorry for himself. 'Oh, go on, Nell,' he complains with a sigh.

Ravian dips his hands back into the soapsuds. He makes a circle between his thumb and forefinger and then blows a perfect bubble.

'Get to work!' Nell hisses in his ear. 'The whole pub is full of empty glasses again.'

She often reminds him how grateful he should be that she gave him a job as a washer-up.

Otherwise, you'd have been a scrawny bag of bones by now, or you'd have had to go out stealing your food. A rat, a robber, a thief! he hears her shouting in his mind.

Ravian throws the tea towel over his shoulder. It stinks of mould and wet dog. Soon his jumper will smell the same. And he's wearing his favourite one today, the one with white and red stripes, especially for his twelfth birthday. Yuck.

He stacks all the glasses from one table in his hand.

'Hey! That one wasn't empty yet!' shouts a man with fiery red hair.

'Yeah, whatever you say,' mutters Ravian.

'Listen, you cheeky little brat,' grumbles the man, 'I said: it wasn't empty yet!'

'Calm down, Rinus. Let the lad do his job,' says a man beside him.

Rinus hits the table with a loud thump. 'Why don't you mind your own business?' He glares at the man and jabs his finger at his face. From a dark corner at the back of the bar comes another voice.

'Hey, ginger, take it easy!'

'What? You too?' Rinus stands up, knocking his chair onto the floor. He's thin and bony and has a bit of a stoop. He stomps past the tables to the dark corner. Everyone is suddenly as quiet as mice, and they're all watching him. He's holding a knife, and he's trying to hide it, but Ravian can still see it. It's gleaming. He's starting to feel nervous, even though it isn't the first time there's been trouble at the pub.

'If you say one more word to me, I'll make the left side of your face just as pretty as the right!' Rinus hisses at the man in the corner, giving him a quick flash of his knife.

Nell yells at them from behind the bar. 'Hey, put your weapons away and stop fighting in my pub! You're like a bunch of children.' Frowning, she shakes her head. Rinus walks back to his table.

'Back to work, you!' Nell shouts at Ravian.

He stacks all the glasses from three tables at once. With the tower of beer glasses leaning against his chest and neck, he tries to clasp three smaller glasses in his other hand.

SMASH!

The three glasses break.

'That's all I need,' says Ravian quietly. Luckily, Nell didn't notice. He puts the stack of unbroken glasses on the bar. Where's the dustpan and brush?

He picks up the pieces with his hands – that'll be faster.

Ow! Blood trickles between his fingers. It's already all over his hand and dripping slowly onto the floor.

'Make sure your boss doesn't see, eh, lad?' says Rinus. 'Or you'll be lucky to make it to your next birthday.'

Ravian stands up and sighs, his shoulders drooping. That's exactly what it is today. His birthday. He throws away the broken glass and carries on as if nothing's wrong. His cut stings in the dirty washing-up water.

'What's all this?!' he suddenly hears from behind him. Nell pulls his hand out of the water.

'Now there's blood in the water! You can't do anything right!'

'I couldn't help it. They just slipped out of my hands. And then I tried –' Ravian says.

'Well, try harder,' she says coldly and gives him an old cloth to bandage the cut.

What does it matter if a glass gets broken now and then?, thinks Ravian. There are so many of them in the pub. Who's going to miss a couple? The boss, of course. She was the one who paid for them.

'Give me another one!' Captain Agnar roars at Ravian, holding up his glass.

Ravian fills it. He's not actually supposed to do that himself, but this man is the captain of the *Devil's Fleet*. Not the sort of person you want to keep waiting for too long.

A fat man with a red face and a grimy shirt suddenly stands up on his chair. There's a big tattoo of a mermaid on his arm. He raises his glass and launches into a shanty.

No wave is too high for us
No distance is too long
No treasure's hidden well enough
No enemy's too strong!

A cross-eyed sailor stands up and joins in.

No ship is too big for us
No peacock could be prouder
No rope can tie us up in knots
And no seagull can screech louder!

The rest of the men at his table stand up and sing along. Soon everyone in the pub is singing together. Ravian has heard this song so many times before.

They're about to get to the bit where everyone sings *yo-ho, yo-ho, yo-hoooo*, badly out of tune.

A man with a black cap and wild eyebrows, who almost tumbled off the stool when he came to sit at the bar, peers at Ravian.

'Why aren't you singing?' he growls. 'You're Lasse's son, aren't you? So that makes you a sailor's son, eh? Hm? Don't you know the words?'

Ravian doesn't reply. Yet another drunkard who can't leave him in peace.

'Seriously? You don't know it?'

Ravian still doesn't reply.

'Well, shame on you!' shouts the man. 'First you start throwing glasses around – and now this! I'm sure your father would be proud.'

Yes, actually, my dad would be proud, thinks Ravian. He thinks it's a stupid song too, and he doesn't sing along with this sort of stuff in harbour pubs. His dad's songs are much better. He wants to say all of that to the man too, but he's not feeling brave enough.

Only one window in the pub has a view of the harbour. During the daytime, there are always men out there, working on and around their ships, with catches of fish being unloaded and lots of shouting. But in the evening, it's always much quieter. Everyone's inside the pub then, warming themselves up, drinking rum and swapping tall stories.

Ravian keeps glancing through the window every couple of minutes. Is he coming?

He doesn't understand. His dad's always around on his birthday. No matter how long he's away, he always comes back on Ravian's birthday. With a big present. While he's gone, Nell keeps an eye on Ravian. At least, that's the idea. But Ravian doesn't really notice her doing much of that.

The sailors in the pub are still singing. Why don't they sing a birthday song for Ravian? Not that Ravian would really want those stupid sailors to sing for him. But it would be nice if at least someone would sing for him today. Actually, though, maybe a whole pub full of people singing for him would be good. And big Captain Agnar could throw him over his shoulder and carry him all around the pub. Everyone would laugh and cheer, and then, to cap it all, Nell would put a big birthday cake on the bar. And Ravian would cut it into slices for everyone and give himself the biggest piece! But how should they know it's his birthday today? No one cares about Ravian, about the little washer-up.

Ravian looks out of the window again. The sun is slowly sinking into the sea. Still no sign of the moss-green sails of his dad's ship. Nothing.

'KLOW! KLIOW!'

It's Marvin! His seagull *and* his best friend. He flies past the pub window and does a flip. Ravian smiles. Marvin knows it's his birthday today. His seagull does another flip. There's something in his beak.

'Could I go outside for a moment?' Ravian asks Nell, who's in a better mood now because someone just told her she has beautiful eyes.

'Go on, but make it quick,' she replies. 'Isn't it about time you started making some normal friends?'

What's she talking about? Marvin is the best friend there is, even if he is a seagull.

Outside, Marvin flies in happy circles around Ravian before perching on his head, with his feet in Ravian's black curls. He gives him what he was holding in his beak. A beautiful big shell, gleaming purplish-green on the inside.

'It's beautiful!' says Ravian. 'This one's going in my collection!'

He keeps all the shells that Marvin has given him in a wooden box.

'Have you seen Dad yet?' Ravian is getting a little nervous now. But he knows he doesn't need to worry about his big, strong dad.

Marvin hangs his head sadly.

'No, eh? But he has to come today, doesn't he?' They look out at the sea together.

'So where's he got to?'

'What did I tell you, you ugly runt?'

When Ravian goes back inside, Rinus is standing in the middle of the pub. He's grabbed the man from the dark corner, the one who insulted him earlier, and he's holding him by the collar.

'The sight of you hurts my eyes!' he yells. He clenches his fist and, with a huge swing, whacks the man on the jaw. The man falls onto the floor, hitting the wall on the way down. A painting tumbles off its hook, right onto his head. He groans. Then he gives

Rinus a hard kick on the shin. Rinus screams and hops up and down. He spits a big slimy blob onto the man's shoulder.

'As ugly as sin. That's what you are!'

Ravian takes a closer look at him now. The man has a big scar right across the right side of his face, from top to bottom. As if someone once slashed him with a knife, or maybe he got it caught on a hook. It looks scary. The skin of the scar is thicker and a paler shade of pink than the rest of his face. It's mean of Rinus to call him as ugly as sin, but Ravian does kind of know what he means.

'Come on, men. What did I say?' Nell shouts as she goes to intervene. 'Sit down, the lot of you! And behave yourselves. You're going to smash up my whole pub!'

The men fall silent. These sailors might be tough, but no one ever dares to argue with Nell. Which is just as well, because otherwise she'd have a hard time in this pub full of rogues.

'Right. Let's drink to peace!' she shouts. The men and Nell knock back glasses of rum.

What a rubbish birthday. Last year Lasse was here, and they had a big party on the beach.

'Nice torches, huh?' Lasse had said, as he made a campfire. 'I bought them from a tribal chief!'

They danced all evening and Lasse played guitar. And he sang his adventuring song. Every single verse of it – and there are loads of them. Ravian knows them all by heart and often sings along, but when he hasn't seen his dad for such a long time, he prefers to keep quiet and listen to him singing. He'd missed him so very much, just as badly as he's missing him now. And after the music Lasse told him stories about his last sea voyage. That was the best thing of all. About far-off islands with big, tall trees, about the huge fishes he caught, and the high waves and the wild storm that almost smashed his ship. And about people who had been at sea for so long that they slowly went mad and forgot how to talk and walk – and even how to sleep.

As Ravian thinks back to his last birthday, it feels like there's a stone in his stomach. He misses Lasse's stories and his jokes and just sitting in silence for hours, the two of them together. If only they could do all those things every day. Ravian has asked so many times why his dad always has to keep going away, but he still doesn't really understand. For the catch, for fishing. But what about Ravian?

'One day you'll be brave enough to go with me,' Lasse always says. But he knows that Ravian is too scared to sail on a ship. They rock and sway, and the sea is unpredictable.

'My little sailor's son who's frightened of boats.'

Ravian sometimes says it out loud. *One day I'll be brave enough.*

Outside, it's slowly getting dark. Inside, the singing is getting louder and louder.

Maybe he's already here, and he'll soon be waiting for me on the beach. Maybe Ravian just didn't notice his dad sailing into the harbour.

But that's impossible. He's been keeping a very close eye on the harbour all day.

It's so dark out there now that the lamps in the harbour are coming on.

'Can I go?' he asks Nell.

'Yes, you little brat,' she snaps.

She thrusts a paper bag into his hands. He always gets some bread and fish to take home after work.

He tosses his apron over the bar and runs off. Outside, Marvin is waiting for him, and he flies into the air as soon as he sees Ravian. Ravian can barely keep up with him. He runs to the dunes just beyond the harbour, to his usual lookout place, where he eats his bread every day. That's where he always stands and watches for his dad approaching in the distance on his birthday. Every year. But it usually happened in the morning. Now it's so dark that even the lamp of the lighthouse has come on.

Ravian holds his hand above his eyes, like sailors do. He doesn't know if you can really see more that way, but it feels like it. Marvin lands on his shoulder. The sea on the horizon has never looked so calm. There's not a single ship in sight.

'He's not coming, Marvin,' says Ravian. 'I think something's really wrong.'

2

THE MAN WITH THE SCAR

In the pitch darkness, Ravian walks home. He has to go through the dunes first, back to the harbour. Marvin flies in silence beside him. The cheerful sound of drunken sailors and clinking glasses is still coming from the pub. Ravian feels as if his feet weigh more than usual. His stomach hurts. What could have happened to his dad? Should he ask for help?

'Maybe I'll just pop back inside to ask around,' Ravian says to Marvin. 'That man with the wild eyebrows knew who my dad is. Maybe that's not all he knows.'

*　*　*

'Ah, look, it's the seagull boy!' shouts Captain Agnar.

'Back already? You're not coming in here with that creature!' snarls Nell.

Marvin flies off Ravian's shoulder and outside. He sits in the open window, so that he can hear what's happening inside.

'Yes, um . . . There was something I wanted to ask,' stammers Ravian. He hesitates for a moment, but then walks purposefully towards the man with the black cap and the wild eyebrows. He's even drunker now and is drooping over the bar like a wet rag. Ravian swallows his nerves.

'Excuse me, sir? You know my father, don't you?'

The man turns around.

'Er, know? I wouldn't say that, but I've met him. Why do you ask?'

'Um, er, well, it's like this . . .'

'Out with it.'

'He didn't come home today.' Ravian tries to look as tough as possible, in spite of the lump in his throat.

'And?' replies the man. 'He's a sailor, isn't he? And sometimes sailors don't come home. That's just how it is. You know that by now, don't you?'

Ravian nods silently and looks around. Who else can he ask?

Captain Agnar? He probably doesn't even know who Ravian's dad is, and he wouldn't tell him anything even if he did know. That dangerous Rinus? Better not. The man with the mermaid tattoo? Too drunk.

'Let me,' says Nell, who heard him asking. Ravian gives her a cautious smile. Sometimes she can be nice.

'Oy, men!' Nell shouts. 'Any of you seen Lasse?'

Everyone turns to look at Ravian. There's a long silence.

'Have you lost him, lad?' someone shouts.

'He was here the other day, wasn't he? With those torches. Yes, and he was looking for you.'

'No,' replies Ravian, 'that was a year ago.'

The men have already stopped paying attention to him. Ravian goes around the pub and asks again at every table. He hesitates before asking the man with the scar, the one who got into a fight with Rinus. Don't stare at it, don't stare at it, don't stare at it . . .

'Sir, you wouldn't happen to know where my father is, would you?'

'No, I don't. And I think there's only one explanation,' the man says seriously. He looks as if he's telling a ghost story. 'He's probably on the ship of . . . Pirate Bank!'

Ravian gasps. A pirate?

'Pirate Bank? Who's that? And why would my dad be with him?'

'Well, my dear boy, Pirate Bank and his ship are cursed. If you board that ship, you'll be stuck there for the rest of your life.'

Ravian stares at the man, eyes wide. A curse? There's no such thing, is there?

'The sea cursed him! As punishment! He's a prisoner on the ship – forever!'

Ravian looks at the man for a long time, and then says, 'Cursed by the sea? Is that possible?'

The man takes a swig of his drink and nods slowly.

'That's not all,' he replies in a mysterious voice. 'She sends sailors on strange courses and tricky routes. She gets them lost and whispers baffling riddles to tell them the way back. No one ever understands her riddles. And she punishes the worst villains with a curse. Which is why Pirate Bank got hit with a pretty nasty one.'

'But why?' asks Ravian.

The man looks around. His scar seems even bigger in the flickering candlelight.

'Well . . . no one knows exactly. But it must have been something terrible, because the sea doesn't get that angry and curse someone like that for no reason.'

'And it's not too hard to imagine Pirate Bank doing something really terrible,' another man agrees.

'I heard Pirate Bank keeps other prisoners on his ship. They have to work for him as slaves! For all eternity!' someone shouts from a corner.

'Just as well Pirate Bank is trapped on the ship!' another man shouts. 'I never dared to moor in a harbour when I saw his ship there. We'd always give it a wide berth and sail on to the next place. Even if it cost us days!'

Ravian fiddles with his sleeve. If these tough sailors are scared of him, then this Bank must be some kind of monster.

'They say he has the devil on his shoulder,' says the man with the scar.

'Wh-what?' stammers Ravian. The men glance at one another. The one with the scar slowly shakes his head.

'Ah, lad, if we told you all the things he's done, you wouldn't be able to sleep for weeks.'

Ravian feels a shiver run up and down his spine. And his dad's with that man? What's going to happen to him?

Then the man with the scar starts roaring with laughter. And so do the men at the next table.

'Oh yes! That's where your father is! That'll be it!' one of them shouts, roaring with laughter.

'If he's been away for so long, it can only be that. He's trapped there! Hahaha!'

Ravian turns around.

'Thanks,' he mumbles, and he heads outside.

Marvin comes towards him.

'Stupid sailors,' whispers Ravian. And he kicks a stone.

He can't stop thinking about it. A cursed ship, a pirate, slaves who have to work for him forever . . . Why else wouldn't Lasse have come home?

Behind the pub is a narrow path that leads to Ravian's house. Not many people know this secret route. It's overgrown with trees and bushes and weeds. It's only a path because Ravian's walked along it so many times that the plants have been permanently flattened.

Halfway along the path lives the Weeping Woman. She's standing on the steps to her front door. She gives him a friendly smile, but she has big purple rings under her eyes, so she looks as if she's just been crying. Ravian used to ask how she was doing, but she always sighed so sadly that he's stopped asking.

'Hello, lad. Have you been at work?' she asks. She blows out a cloud of cigarette smoke.

'Yes, it was busy again.'

'Saturday, eh?' she says. She gives him a wave and heads into her house.

'Excuse me?' Ravian calls after her. 'Have you seen my dad today? Did you see him come home?'

'Oh, lad,' says the Weeping Woman. 'No, I haven't seen anything, but I've been busy all day. Maybe he's already in the house.'

Ravian looks at their little white house in the distance. There's no light. No one at home.

'Thank you,' he says quietly, and he walks on before the woman can start crying.

The house is filled with the cold air of disappointment. It doesn't have any separate rooms. It's just one big space. Ravian and Lasse sleep on a mattress in the middle of the floor. That's where they eat too and play card games. When Lasse's not at home, Ravian has the whole mattress to himself.

Everything looks just the same as before. On the mattress, the blankets are exactly as Ravian left them after kicking them off this morning. The chest in the corner with his clothes in is still open. The old box with the purple cushion where Marvin sleeps is full of feathers and sand. Ravian isn't very good at cleaning. But that's because it's so boring. That's the one good thing about his dad not being there – Ravian never has to tidy up. There's a lot of washing-up to do too. He'd meant to do it all before his dad got home, but he forgot. And now it doesn't matter.

'Come on, Marvin. Shall we pretend the bed's our ship again? Or do you want to sail in your box and follow my big ship? We can be a fleet!'

Marvin flies straight to his box and gets ready for the adventure.

Ravian throws his blanket over the mantlepiece, which is behind the mattress.

'That's the sail,' he explains, 'and the floor is the sea.'

He holds his hand up to his eye as a telescope.

'Look, Sailor Marvin, there's a whale in the distance!'

Marvin flaps into the air and gives a happy squawk.

'Quick! Let's sail over there! Maybe the whale can help us to find Dad! Whale! Whale! Hey, wait a moment, whale!'

Ravian shakes his blanket.

'Wind in the sails! Ahoooooy!'

Marvin shrieks and points his wing at a chair by the wall.

'Oh no!' shouts Ravian. 'A pirate ship! Well spotted, sailor. Load the cannons!'

He sits down on the mattress and takes off a sock.

'FIRE!' he yells, throwing his sock at the chair. It's a miss.

'More cannonballs!' He throws his other sock too. Hit!

'Ha! Stupid pirates!' he yells, falling exhausted onto his back.

Marvin lands back in his box. Ravian pulls the blanket over himself.

'Marvin? Do you think . . .' he begins.

He sighs.

'Want to go stargazing?' he says finally.

He stands up and puts on his coat. Marvin is already at the door.

Next to the house is a small dip in the dunes. Ravian lies down with his arms behind his head, so he won't get any sand in his black curls.

'It's nearly full.' Ravian points at the moon. 'Makes it harder to see the stars.' Marvin looks up.

'We taught those pirates a lesson, didn't we?' Ravian says happily. Then they both sit in silence.

'You don't really think Dad's with a pirate, do you? On a cursed ship?' he says after a while. 'They were just joking, weren't they?'

They listen to the sea. Ravian can feel his tummy churning with anxiety. The devil on his shoulder, he thinks to himself. What if Lasse really is trapped there? Or maybe he was trapped there, but then the pirate threw him overboard, or perhaps he escaped by jumping into the sea. Maybe drowning was better than staying on board with the pirate. But if the curse is real, he wouldn't even be able to jump overboard. That thought makes Ravian feel sick.

'Do you think the pirate really exists, Marvin? Why would that man have started talking about him if he didn't?'

As he looks up at the sky, he thinks about how very far away the stars are. The sea is at least as deep. What would Ravian do if his dad was at the bottom of it? He sits up.

'Marvin, I think we need to go in search of this pirate. I don't know if Dad's really with him, but it's worth a try, isn't it?'

Marvin makes a hesitant little sound.

'Yes, I know the man with the frightening scar said you can never get off the ship again. But maybe we can just shout from the quayside and ask if Dad's on board. And then rescue him without going on board ourselves. And you know I don't really like going on ships anyway. That curse has to be fake, and if it's not, I'll get it lifted somehow. I'm sure I can do that with help from you and Dad.'

Ravian stands up and brushes the sand off his bum.

'Come on, Marvin, I'll go and ask where we can find this Pirate Bank.'

Marvin doesn't move a feather.

'I'm going anyway, Marvin. And I need you,' says Ravian. 'Will you help me? Please?'

Marvin flies up and sits in his usual spot on Ravian's shoulder.

* * *

They walk along the secret path and back to the pub. The lights are out at the Weeping Woman's house. Ravian hopes she's having a happy dream.

From a distance, the pub seems quieter now. It's really late.

'They probably won't be very pleased to see me again,' says Ravian.

But before he reaches the door, a man comes out. He's wearing a big black cloak, which he flings around his shoulders. It's the man with the scar!

'Sir! Sir, can I ask you something?' Ravian hurries over to him and gives his cloak a cautious tug.

The man looks around. He's breathing heavily.

'Huh? Oh, it's you again. What do you want?' he growls as he strides off.

Ravian races after him. He hardly dares to ask. The man will probably say he made it all up, and it's just some old ghost story. He'll probably laugh at him. But actually, Ravian doesn't care. He needs to know for sure.

'Pirate Bank,' says Ravian. 'Where can I find him?'

The man stops now and peers at him. He looks at Ravian, then Marvin and back again. Then he looks at the sea. The flash of the lighthouse sweeps across his face, making it seem even scarier than before. It's as if a big fat worm ate its way out from under his skin. Ravian shudders.

'I was joking, lad,' the man says gruffly, walking on.

'Yes, but I still want to go and look for him. What if you were right?'

'I wasn't. And it's far too dangerous.'

'I can decide that for myself,' says Ravian, sounding tougher than he feels and holding on to the man's cloak to stop him. The man glares at Ravian.

'So, does Pirate Bank really exist?' asks Ravian.

'Yes, of course he really exists. I've seen him with my own two eyes.' He gulps. 'Lad, it really is far too dangerous for the likes of you.'

'Please! Tell me where to find him!' says Ravian, staring at him.

With a sigh, the man replies, 'Well, my friend, it's up to you.'

He crouches down so that he can look Ravian straight in the eye.

'Pirate Bank and his cursed ship hardly ever moor,' he whispers. 'Only at full moon. Then he calls in briefly at Deaf Diederik's harbour. That's not far from here, two days' walk to the north. He comes to stock up on fresh supplies of rum and food.'

He takes Ravian by the shoulder. His breath stinks. Ravian blinks. He doesn't want to go looking for the scary pirate – no way! But he has no choice. He has to do it. For his dad. Before it's too late.

'And whatever you do,' the man continues, 'don't go on board.'

He stands up and walks away. Then he turns around, one last time.

'Don't say I didn't warn you!'

3

THE JOURNEY TO DEAF DIEDERIK'S HARBOUR

'This one or this one?' Ravian holds up two jumpers, both striped, and looks at Marvin. 'This one's warmer, but the other one's clean.'

Ravian shrugs and stuffs them both into his backpack. If he keeps himself busy packing, then he won't have to think about the danger that's ahead. Then he won't have to feel how scared he really is. Scared of the pirate, scared of his ship, and maybe most scared of all that he won't find his dad. Nervously, he grabs a few more things: a box of matches, an exciting book with a picture of a lighthouse and a girl on the front, and a rope.

'Oh, and a pair of dry socks. For if I get wet feet. There's nothing worse than that. Wet feet.'

Marvin just laughs. A big cackling laugh with his beak wide open.

'Yes, your feet like to splash around, Marvin, but mine don't!'

His backpack is almost full. He throws in a couple of apples and some bread.

'What have we forgotten?' Ravian checks all the shelves in the cupboard. In the middle on a high shelf there's a case. It belongs to Lasse.

'Maybe there's something useful in there,' Ravian mumbles.

The case contains a few notes, a pine cone, an old dark-red handkerchief, three walnuts and a compass.

'Oh, that could come in handy.' He takes the compass from the case. It's silver and it hangs on a long chain. Ravian puts it with his backpack, so that he can wear it around his neck tomorrow. He knots the handkerchief around his head.

'Hey, Marvin. I look just like a scary pirate, don't I? I'm sure Pirate Bank is going to fall for it,' says Ravian with a smile.

Marvin shakes his head.

Ravian also has serious doubts when he sees his reflection in the window. He sighs in disappointment. His heart sinks for a moment. There's nothing dangerous about him. He looks like a helpless little boy who is searching for his dad. But that's exactly what he is. Although he doesn't feel as small as he looks. He takes a deep breath and puffs out his chest.

'We're leaving early tomorrow morning. The man with the scar said it's two days' walk.' Ravian looks at the dark sky. 'Then it'll be exactly full moon when we get there. But first we need to sleep,' he says quietly, blowing out the candle. 'We'll get up with the sun, okay?'

Marvin lies nice and snug in his old box with his eyes closed. Seagulls don't really snore, but their breath sometimes makes a lot of noise when they're sleeping. You can hear their beaks chattering.

Ravian lies in bed, listening to his sleeping friend. He hopes that if he just concentrates on the sound, it'll calm him down and help him to sleep. But it doesn't work. He tosses and turns. His blanket is too warm, but without a blanket it's too cold. He slides his foot off the mattress because it's more comfortable, but every time he's about to drift off to sleep, he dreams that the mattress is a boat and his foot is dangling in the sea. Then he awakes with a start.

Dad. A pirate. A cursed ship. What's he supposed to do when he reaches the ship? With his fear of boats? How will he ever get Lasse off Pirate Bank's ship?

It's an hour before he finally falls asleep, so tired after all his worrying.

In the fresh morning air, they set off on their way. Ravian has hung the compass around his neck, under his shirt. It looks pretty expensive, so he doesn't want anyone to see it. He yawns, rubs the sleep from his eyes, throws some water in his face and slaps himself on the cheeks. Come on. This is where the adventure begins. You can do it. He ties the handkerchief around his head again and thinks about how tough his dad is. If Lasse is tough, then Ravian must take after him. So he is too. From now on. Yes, from now on, he'll be tough.

They head along their familiar path towards the harbour of Rottenherring. From there, they need to head north.

The Weeping Woman is outside again, hanging her washing on a long line in the garden. It looks so lovely and peaceful, those long white dresses fluttering in the breeze.

'Hey!' she calls out to Ravian.

'Morning,' he shouts back.

'Where are you off to with your backpack?'

'To look for my dad!'

'Oh, has he still not come home?'

'No, that's why I'm searching for him.'

'Yes, I understood that much. But where?'

Ravian looks around before going closer.

'I'm going to find Pirate Bank. I think my dad's on board his ship.'

The woman gasps. Her eyes fill with tears, and she claps a hand over her mouth.

'Ravian, would you like a cup of tea? Inside the house?'

He gets goosebumps. So she knows the stories about Pirate Bank too. Why does everyone suddenly seem to have heard of him? Should Ravian be as worried as she is? Ravian doesn't really have time, but it might be a good idea to have a chat with her. And tea does sound nice.

'Just a quick one,' he says, following her inside.

Her house is painted dark yellow, inside and out. Small fish and big fish, in green and blue and purple, are painted on the walls of the kitchen and the living room. Her curtains are made of strings of shells.

Ravian sits down at the table and the woman makes him a cup of hot tea with honey. Then she puts a delicious-smelling plate of warm yellow things in front of him.

'What are those?' asks Ravian.

'Chestnuts, from the garden. I just roasted them. Try one.'

Ravian takes a bite. 'They're so good!' he cries, quickly taking another one.

The Weeping Woman laughs.

'You look just like your dad with that handkerchief on your head,' she says. 'He used to wear one too. A long time before you were born, he used to walk along that path. His hair is much lighter than yours, of course, and he doesn't have such lovely freckles, but with that handkerchief you're just like each other.'

Ravian smiles.

'Did he ever come round for tea?' he asks.

'Yes, he often used to pay us a visit.'

'Us?'

'I used to live here with my husband,' says the woman quietly, staring outside.

'Your husband? So . . . Where is he now?' asks Ravian. But she doesn't reply.

'You're off to look for a pirate, then, are you?' she says suddenly. 'All on your own?'

'No,' Ravian replies with his mouth full. 'With Marvin.'

Marvin is sitting on the back of an empty chair with his eyes contentedly shut.

The woman frowns. 'Ah, I see . . .'

But then Ravian jumps to his feet and says in a cheerful voice, 'Right, we really need to get going. Thanks for the chestnuts!'

'Take a few with you.' The woman stands up and fills a paper bag for him. 'I've got enough, and they're really good for you, particularly if you're going on a long journey.'

When Ravian goes to take the paper bag from her, she holds on to it. She looks at him for a long time with her watery eyes. 'Are you absolutely sure about this?'

Ravian nods confidently. But a little voice, far away in the back of his head, is squeaking at him to stay.

With the Weeping Woman and her dancing washing and her hot tea.

'But . . . Pirate Bank . . . D-do you know what he . . .' she stammers. She almost seems to be getting angry.

'Don't worry,' Ravian says, interrupting her before she can change his mind and that squeaky little voice wins. 'In four days' time, I'll be back here. I hope. Two days there, two days back. I'll be with my dad. And we'll come to visit you. I'm sure he'll have missed you.'

Ravian takes the bag of chestnuts from her hand and puts it in his backpack.

Then the Weeping Woman falls to her knees and throws her arms around him.

'Please, Ravian . . .'

Ravian wriggles out of her grasp. He doesn't want to hear what she has to say. Why is she acting so strangely? Doesn't she think he can go on a journey? Or have an adventure without dying within five minutes? Who does she think she is? His mother?

'Yes, yes! I'll be careful. I promise!' he calls as he walks back out through the door to the path, with Marvin on his shoulder. 'And thanks!' He waves without looking back at her.

The Weeping Woman stands on the steps and watches him go until she can't see him any more.

'That blasted sea takes everyone away from me,' she sobs quietly.

At the harbour, Ravian glances over at the pub, which is closed now. Nell will probably be angry at him for not coming into work for a few days without any notice. She'll have to wash all the glasses herself. Oh, he can worry about that later. She'll understand that this is more important.

He takes his compass out from under his jumper and places it flat on the palm of his hand. That's what you have to do, or it won't work. He learned that from Lasse.

'You need to make sure that the red arrow is pointing to N for North . . .' He turns his body a little to the right. 'And then we have to walk in that direction. It's actually very simple.'

He puts the compass away and starts striding in the right direction. Marvin flies beside him.

'When I was little,' Ravian chuckles, 'I thought the arrow of a compass always pointed to Dad. That would be pretty handy now, wouldn't it?'

In silence, the two friends travel on, at first through the dunes they know so well, where they've been for lots of long walks. But in the distance they can see a forest of tall dark trees, which they'll have to pass through soon. And that's new territory. Ravian glances back now and then to check that he can see his house. He can still go back . . . But he quickly shakes off that thought. No, we're not going back. If Dad turns out not to be with that pirate, we'll be back here before we know it. He looks at Marvin, who returns his look, encouragingly. It's still early in the day, and it won't be dark for a long time. Off we go on our adventure, thinks Ravian.

*   *   *

The forest has a clear beginning. First, they cross the heathland for a really long time, and then suddenly there are trees all around. Ravian pauses for a moment and looks up at the tops of the trees. He has to tilt his head all the way back. With his heavy backpack on, he almost falls over.

'Wow . . .' he says quietly.

There isn't really a path. The trees are close together and Marvin has to keep flying really low.

'Watch out for those overhanging branches, won't you?' says Ravian. 'Some of them don't have any leaves, so they're harder to spot.' Marvin nimbly flies over and under the branches.

On the ground are leaves and branches that rustle and snap when Ravian steps on them. Otherwise, it's spookily quiet. He's used to always being able to hear the murmur of the sea, even when there's no other sound at all. But now the sea is too far away.

'Shall we sing a song?'

'MEE, MEE.'

'Dad's adventuring song?'

Marvin nods.

'Let's do the bit about the haunted wood.'

Ravian starts singing. Marvin squawks along.

In the forest of the night,
The haunted wood, the haunted wood!
Where the branches on the trees
Seem to whisper on the breeze
And the bushes full of leaves
Are a home for ghosts and thieves
But we're strong and safe and sound
And we'll firmly stand our ground (**KLOW KLOW**)
In the forest of the night.

In the forest of the night
The haunted wood, the haunted wood!
Where creatures howl and bite

Oh, but they won't give us a fright (**KLOW KLOW**)
In the forest of the night

When you're laughing and singing a lot, a journey goes pretty fast. Ravian forgets his worries and his nerves for a little while. Then it starts to get dark. As the sun goes lower, the forest becomes darker, but he can still see well enough. He goes on humming the tune, to chase away the silence.

Then they hear a loud bang. It sounds like a big branch breaking. Ravian freezes.

Startled, he stops in his tracks and whispers, 'What was that?'

They hear more branches snapping, somewhere up in the trees.

'Marvin?'

In the distance, there's a low growling.

Is this really a haunted forest?

Ravian holds his breath. The growl is getting louder and louder.

Marvin has perched on a branch and is sitting there, as quiet as a mouse. He peers around with wide eyes, a very focused look on his face.

Ravian glances up at his friend. What *is* that noise? Could it be a wild animal?

Then there's another sound. It's coming closer and closer, but Ravian can't tell what it is. The trees are close together and the leaves are so dark that Ravian can't see very far. *Woohoooo*. A big brown bird flies low over him. He feels the blasts of wind from its powerful wingbeats. Its claws graze the top of Ravian's head, just lightly. Ravian holds on to the handkerchief so that he doesn't lose it. The bird flaps its wings up and down a few times and disappears. Ravian watches it go. Phew! It was just an owl.

Ravian's relief doesn't last long. The growling is still there. He hardly dares, but for a moment he squeezes his eyes tightly shut so he'll have a better chance of hearing where the sound is coming from. The growling is coming from the left, and it seems to be getting closer. It sounds more like roaring now. Slow and low. He can hear branches and twigs cracking. Something's there. And that something isn't happy that Ravian's come to visit.

He feels his heart pounding faster and faster. His breath is getting quicker. Is it fear? Or is it because he's trying to hold it in? Lasse once told him that if you meet a wild animal, you have to pretend to be dead. Then the animal thinks that it doesn't have to bother killing you. Ravian's forehead starts to sweat. He knows all that, but how do you pretend to be dead? The animal would know you were pretending, wouldn't it? Particularly if your heart was beating away like this . . .

Ravian very calmly drops down onto his knees and then onto his bum. He's moving so slowly that he's like a tortoise. And then, very carefully, he lies on his side. His backpack is in the way, but he keeps it on. The growling is still coming from the bushes. Ravian picks up a big stick that's lying nearby. At least he'll have a weapon at the ready. He lies there for a while, listening to the growls. He imagines the scariest monsters, but that makes him so terrified that he tries to think about something else. He looks up at Marvin, who's sitting perfectly still on his branch. As if he's stuffed.

Then the growling stops. It's silent. Dead silent.

'GEP GEP GEP!' Marvin squawks, flying into the air. From the bushes, a big animal on four hairy legs comes running, with more growling and barking. It's a wolf!

AWOOOO, the animal howls, heading straight for Ravian, who squeezes his eyes shut and lies still. Pretend you're dead, pretend you're dead. When the beast reaches Ravian and sees him lying there, it comes to a stop. Its mouth drooling, it sniffs at Ravian's arm, his shoulder and then his face. The animal gives a disappointed whine, turns around and, hanging its head, walks back to the bushes. Ravian lies there for a little longer, breathing in and out, now that he's able to breathe properly again. Then he sits up – and the twigs beneath him quietly snap.

The wolf pricks up its ears. Howling, it turns around. The beast's lip curls and, with a growl, it shows its sharp fangs. It races towards Ravian. Ravian's heart thumps even faster. He can't think clearly. How could he have been so stupid? As the wolf comes closer and closer, Ravian knows no one can help him. Is he never going to see his father again? Dad! He jumps to his feet, grabs the big stick, and throws it as far as he can into the bushes. The wolf watches the stick go, gives a happy bark and races after it.

'Go!' Ravian shouts at Marvin. The seagull flies into the air and, without looking back, Ravian runs away from the wolf as fast as he can. After a while, he's exhausted, and he leans against a tree to catch his breath.

'Wolves . . . they're actually just big dogs,' he says casually. But for the rest of the journey, he keeps glancing at the bushes out of the corner of his eye.

As they walk on, the forest becomes really dark.

'Maybe we should stop for the night, Marvin,' says Ravian. 'Look, a clearing. Let's go over there.'

There are no trees in the clearing, just moss and grass, and it's illuminated by the bright moon.

'Okay, Marvin, we need to make a campfire. Dad's taught me that it keeps wild animals away. Sounds a bit odd to me – wouldn't wild animals want to warm themselves up too? I'm going to look for some big branches. Could you fetch some twigs? And a bit of dry moss? That'll make the fire easier to light.

When they've gathered everything, Ravian piles the moss and the twigs and stacks the branches around them like a kind of tent. He lights the moss with a match. Before long, it's blazing away, and the branches catch fire too. Ravian keeps one big piece of wood close at hand, so that he can grab it quickly. You never know . . .

'Cosy, eh?' Ravian says to Marvin, who has come to sit close to the fire and is staring into the flames. 'Want a chestnut?'

The two friends sit there together, feeling nice and warm as they nibble on the chestnuts.

'We should take it in turns to sleep because the fire has to stay lit. And we also need to be on the lookout. What if a lion suddenly appears, and it *would* like to sit by the fire?'

Marvin laughs, quietly chattering with his beak.

'Yeah, okay, maybe not a lion, but perhaps a lynx, or a bear. Or that wolf.'

Ravian prods the fire with a long stick.

'You go to sleep. I'll take the first watch,' he says. Every creak in the bushes and every gust of wind gives him a bit of a fright. What's that moving out there? He keeps his hand safely on the big piece of wood. It's probably nothing. Or has the wolf followed them?

Marvin soon dozes off. Ravian concentrates on the flames and how they're moving. He quietly sings a bit of his dad's adventuring song, to keep himself awake.

But we're strong and safe and sound
And we'll firmly stand our ground

The fire crackles peacefully.

I'll see Dad again tomorrow, he thinks. The long, hard walk, the songs and the wolf had almost made him forget to miss his father. He really hopes his dad isn't locked up in a cell as Bank's prisoner. He hopes the notorious pirate is a little bit friendly. Does such a thing exist? A friendly pirate? That's another of those questions that only his dad has the answer to. But maybe his dad isn't on that ship at all, and then he doesn't need to worry about such things. Maybe he's somewhere playing the guitar and singing songs. By a campfire, like Ravian and Marvin.

When the fire starts to die down, Ravian throws another piece of wood on it and gives Marvin a prod. 'Your turn!'

Shivering, Ravian stirs as the sun rises. The fire has gone out and Marvin is lying beside it, fast asleep.

'Marvin!' shouts Ravian.

The seagull wakes up with a start.

'You were supposed to stay awake because I was asleep!'

'**MEEEE,**' replies Marvin, looking very sorry.

'Well, luckily nothing bad happened. You dozy bird.'

Ravian gives Marvin a nudge and then takes an apple from his backpack. After six big bites, he throws the core into the air, where Marvin catches it.

'Right, now we've both had breakfast. Let's get going.' He takes out his compass. 'This way!'

After a long walk, they leave the forest and finally see dunes again. They're different dunes from the ones at home – very rough-looking, with lots of prickly plants and dark bushes. The tops of the dunes are higher, and the dips are deeper.

'They're like mountains, Marvin,' says Ravian. But he knows there are no mountains around here. 'Maybe I'm the first person to discover that there are actually mountains in this country. I'm sure the people in the pub will be interested to hear about that. Maybe they'll finally listen to what I have to say.'

'Look, we're nearly at the beach!' Ravian shouts a little later, when the friends have crossed the dunes. 'If we just keep following the coast, we'll eventually come to Deaf Diederik's harbour!'

But when they get to the sea, they find that it's not a beach. It's just a lot of big rocks with sharp edges and slippery tops.

'The waves are so high here,' Ravian murmurs. 'The sea's never this wild at home.' He looks at Marvin.

'I'm not going over those rocks – I'll slip and fall. I'd better keep on walking along this last line of dunes. Then I can still follow the coast, but my feet will stay dry. What do you think, Marvin?'

Ravian turns around and climbs back up the dune. He wonders if his dad would have done the same.

But Dad likes getting his feet wet, Ravian thinks, so that's not fair.

The path through the dunes keeps taking Ravian a little away from the sea and then back again. The sun turns orange and then almost red. It makes the sky look like a painting, which is beautiful, but it also means that the sun's about to go down.

'Where's this harbour?' Ravian shouts into the wind. They haven't travelled all this way for nothing, have they?

The path has been leading inland and away from the sea for a long time now. Ravian takes out his compass. Is he still heading north? Not quite. He leaves the path and heads straight towards the north again. Marvin flies above him. It gets dark.

Without a path and without light, climbing back up the dune is pretty tricky. As long as he can hear the sea on the other side, Ravian knows it's okay. And Marvin will squawk if he sees anything.

Marvin starts shrieking. **'GEP GEP GEP GEP!'**

'What is it, Marvin?' Ravian looks up. 'Can you see the harbour?'

Marvin makes happy sounds and starts flying faster towards the sea.

Ravian runs after him, climbing up the dunes through the prickly bushes. The moon is now above the sea and shining brightly. The water is like silver.

'But I can't see any sign of ships,' says Ravian. 'Or a harbour either.'

Marvin gives a loud squawk and points with his wing into the distance.

Ravian narrows his eyes. And he can see a small bay, still far away. And a light.

'Is that it?' says Ravian in surprise. 'That place looks so small!' Then he thinks about it. 'Yes, it'd be the perfect hideout for a pirate.'

As they get closer, Ravian sees that the light isn't coming from the harbour but from the big ship that's moored there. And there's a tune coming from the ship.

It's his dad's adventuring song!

4

THE *NIGHT RAIDER*

In Deaf Diederik's harbour, they find a crumbling wall. Ravian hides behind the wall while Marvin stands on it. There are lots of cracks and holes that Ravian can peep through to see what's happening in the harbour. The harbour's misty, so it's hard to get a good view of the ship.

'Yes, up here. Give it a good shove!' growls a voice from the ship. Ravian can't see who the voice belongs to, just the dark figure of a man.

He hears the clinking of bottles. Another man is pushing a big wooden crate up the gangplank from the quayside and onto the ship.

'Careful! Stop there,' the growling voice says threateningly when the crate reaches the ship.

The man doesn't reply, just walks back down the gangplank to fetch another crate.

The waves make an incredible noise as they hit the sides of the ship. The next crate is pushed up the gangplank, the wood squeaking.

'Thank you. You will be careful, won't you?' That's a different voice. It sounds much friendlier and a little higher than the other one. Younger.

The man who pushed the crate walks away again without replying and fetches another crate.

Very quietly now, but still clearly, Ravian hears that familiar tune again.

'Can you hear that?' he says to Marvin, stepping out from behind the wall.

As he comes closer to the ship, he can make out the words.

Where the branches on the trees

Seem to whisper on the breeze . . .

He can hear it so clearly now. There's no doubt about it. It's Lasse!

Closer to the ship, there's a post for Ravian to hide behind. But he needs to show himself if he wants to save his dad. Marvin flies to join him. They watch as the last crate is pushed up the gangplank. No one says anything this time.

'That man pushing the crate up to the ship must be Deaf Diederik,' whispers Ravian. Marvin, sitting on top of the post, nods in agreement. 'It's funny that they're talking to him even though he doesn't seem to be able to hear them.'

As Deaf Diederik heads into the harbourmaster's house, Ravian knows he'll have to be quick, before they pull up the gangplank again and head out to sea for another month. But he doesn't dare to step out into the open. What's he going to say if someone sees him?

Rav . . . Rav, I'm here! He suddenly hears his dad calling from the ship. *Ravian, have you come to rescue me?*

Ravian stops thinking about it. He stands up and runs straight towards the ship.

Close up, it looks even bigger. The masts rise into the sky like towering trees. The sails are dark and all four of them are much bigger than any sails Ravian has ever seen before. The gangplank from the ship to the quayside has clearly not seen much use, only for the crates. It looks brand-new, in fact. Around the ship is a thick mist with a strange purple glow. The wind blows hard through Ravian's curls and through the ship's rigging. It seems to be howling, like the wolf in the forest. The wooden boards creak as the dark figure walks across the deck with slow, heavy steps. Ravian looks around. There's no sign now of Deaf Diederik, or whoever it was. The waves wash over the quayside, bringing a cold stench of fish and seaweed.

The dark figure seems to have gone. Ravian can't see or hear him. Now he's all alone in the cold, cold harbour. Just him and Marvin, who's floating on the wind above Ravian's head.

'Dad? Are you there?' Ravian whispers as loud as he can.

For a moment, there's silence.

Yes, Ravian, I'm on the ship!

The ship is rocking on the waves. The ropes along the rail slap against the side of the ship with loud thuds. Ravian gulps.

'Dad, I'm coming!' he says, taking a step towards the gangplank. But then he stops. The ship's moving so wildly . . . What on earth was he thinking? He doesn't even dare to go on his dad's fishing boat, and now he's planning to run onto a cursed pirate ship? He looks at the wild waves. His head is spinning and it feels as if he's slipping out of his own body. But he places one hesitant foot on the gangplank. For Lasse.

'Hey, who's there?'

Ravian gasps. His back is drenched with sweat.

'I heard someone down there, didn't I?' the voice from the ship says. 'Hello?'

Should Ravian answer or hide again? 'Um . . .' he begins.

'Well? Who are you?'

It doesn't sound angry, more like quiet and curious. Now Ravian recognises the friendly voice from before.

He takes a deep breath. 'I . . . I'm Lasse's son. I've come to fetch him.'

A face appears in the dim light. It's a boy with blond hair. To Ravian's surprise, he's not much older than Ravian himself. He has red cheeks, and he's wearing a thick blue jumper.

'Okay,' says the boy calmly. 'Who's Lasse?'

'My father,' says Ravian.

'Yes, you said you're his son. But why have you come to fetch him?'

'Because I want him to come home, of course.'

'But where is he? Where are you trying to fetch him from?'

Ravian frowns. The boy's playing some silly game. What's he doing on that ghost ship anyway? And where's the pirate?

'He's a prisoner on your ship! And I'm here to take him home!' Ravian still doesn't have a clue how exactly he's going to do that, but he thinks he's made a pretty good job of sounding like he knows what he's doing.

'There aren't any prisoners on this ship,' says the boy. 'Except for me. And the pirate, but that's where it all started, of course.' Ravian gives him a confused look.

'And other than that, there's no one here at all.' The boy says it so simply that Ravian's not sure whether to believe him.

'Are you trying to make a fool of me?' Ravian asks irritably.

'No, absolutely not. I swear it!'

'But I just heard my dad, didn't I? I heard him calling, and I heard a song that only he and I know!'

The blond boy sighs and looks back at the ship.

Ravian! Ravian!

'You see? I really can hear it! Even down here on the quayside!' says Ravian.

He takes another step onto the gangplank. And another.

'No, stop! Be careful!' the boy shouts, suddenly seeming to panic. 'There's something you need to know.'

He looks very serious now. 'You really need to stop there and, seriously, stop walking as I'm telling you the story.' The boy looks at Ravian, a pleading expression on his face. 'And you have to believe me and trust me.'

Ravian raises an eyebrow. 'About the curse? Yes, I know about that already,' he says boldly, taking another step. 'But I don't believe a word of it.'

'Stop!' the boy says, shouting so loud that his voice cracks. 'Do you think I'm here for fun? On this ship? With that pirate? Do you think this is what I wanted for myself?'

Ravian stands still again. Maybe it is true.

'So there really is a curse?' he asks.

The sea is even wilder now. The ship is rocking even more violently. A wave washes over the gangplank, and it shakes and wobbles under Ravian's feet. He shivers and feels everything spinning as he looks at the raging water. He takes a step back. Maybe he should just stay on the safe quayside after all.

The boy on the ship nods sadly.

'Yes, really,' he says. 'Your father isn't here. And if he was, do you think he'd want to stay of his own free will?' He's talking louder and louder. 'On a ship with a pirate? Instead of going home? Going home to you?'

Rav . . . Ravi . . . Don't give up! There's Lasse's voice again. The louder the waves crash, the louder he shouts.

'He *is* here!' shouts Ravian, really angrily now. 'I almost believed you!'

And he runs up the gangplank. His feet don't have a good grip on the wet wood, and they almost slip from under him. If he runs fast enough, he won't fall. But the wood at the top is even more slippery. Ravian's nearly there. But then his foot slips off the plank, and he falls forward onto his chin. His left arm and his legs are dangling from the gangplank. Just in time, a strong hand grasps his arm and pulls him back to safety.

Ravian lies panting as he looks down at the water beneath him. His stomach flips when he sees the sea. His head is thumping from the whack under his chin. He's got a nasty cut – he can feel it stinging. When he looks up, he sees the boy peering at him from the deck, with a worried expression on his face. Ravian stands up straight on the gangplank again and the boy slowly lets go of him. He wipes some muck off Ravian's jumper. 'Thank you,' mumbles Ravian, still out of breath.

Behind the boy, he now sees the deck of the ship, which is lit by a single flame. The crates that were just taken on board are stacked in a corner. The bottles of rum are clinking. There's no sign of the pirate.

Ravian places one hand on the rail and leans forward to see more of the ship.

The boy grabs his arm again, but this time it feels insistent.

He stares hard at Ravian, as if he's trying to tell him something with his eyes.

'I'm Kars,' he says then. 'You don't know me, and I don't know you. But I'm trying to protect you. Like I did just now.' He gently pushes Ravian away from him. 'You mustn't walk any further. Please.'

Ravian looks at Kars's face. It's dirty, with black smudges and dust. He has a scar over his eyebrow.

'I wish someone had warned me before I came on board,' he says quietly. 'I've been here for more than a year now.'

Ravian doesn't know what to do. He hesitates. He really did hear his dad. But he believes Kars. That curse might well exist, but his dad must be here too.

'I'm Ravian,' he says.

'Hello, Ravian.' Kars lessens his grip.

'That's Marvin.' Ravian points at the sky.

'Who?'

'The seagull.'

'Ah, okay. Hi, Marvin,' says Kars with a grin.

Marvin flies down to perch on Ravian's shoulder. **'KLOW!'** he says.

Kars takes his hand off Ravian's arm. The wind starts blowing harder, and the sea swirls and pounds even more wildly than before.

Rav! Help me!

His dad's voice is clearer than ever.

'Dad!' he shouts back.

Kars looks at him in confusion, as if Ravian is speaking a language he doesn't understand.

Ravian looks at Marvin. He'll understand.

But Marvin is looking at him with a puzzled expression too. 'You can hear Dad shouting, can't you, Marvin?'

'Is he calling you now?' asks Kars.

'Yes! It's really loud! Listen!' snaps Ravian.

Kars looks over the rail at the foaming waves.

'Oh yes, that'll be it . . .' he mumbles.

'What?' shouts Ravian. He has tears in his eyes. The wind is blowing harder and harder, biting into Ravian's cheeks. 'Do you think I'm mad? It's my dad! Don't you think I'd recognise his voice better than anyone else?'

Ravian, you can do it. Come here, to me. Then we'll be together again!

Lasse sounds so comforting and warm. No one understands Ravian like he does.

'I'm coming, Dad!' he says, and he lifts one foot to step onto the boat.

'No! Don't do it!' yells Kars, grabbing Ravian by the shoulders.

Marvin flies up with a worried screech.

'Let go of me!' sobs Ravian. 'If that stupid curse really does exist, then at least I'll always be together with my dad!'

And taking one big step, he jumps on board.

With a dull thud, he lands on the deck.

And then all the sounds disappear for a moment.

He can't hear the wind any more, he can't hear the waves, he can't hear the planks creaking or the bottles clinking. Silence.

Ravian stands motionless, looking around. He hears a bang, somewhere very close but high in the air. And then there's a flash. Angry raindrops pelt down onto the ship and the boys. The wind blows harder than Ravian has ever known, and the purple strands of mist swirl violently. The rigging clatters, the sails rattle, and the waves smash against the ship.

Kars covers his face with his hands and sinks to the deck, defeated.

Marvin gives a panicked shriek and tries hard not to get blown away.

'Dad?' Ravian shouts through the thunder.

But he doesn't hear an answer.

'Dad? I'm here! Where are you?'

But all Ravian hears is the rain and the storm.

5

THE CURSE

'Dad?'

Ravian feels like he's been shouting for hours. The rocking of the boat is making him feel sick, and the rain has soaked right through him too. He longs to hear the voice that just called to him.

'Dad, why won't you answer?'

He paces across the deck. Did the voice come from the left? Or from the right? Or was it more from the back of the boat?

'Hey,' he says to Kars, who is still sitting on the deck and watching in silence. 'Don't just sit there. Why don't you help me?'

Kars shrugs and sighs.

'I can't help you. He's not here. I already told you that.'

Ravian frowns.

'Then isn't it a bit strange that I just heard him?'

'And isn't it a bit strange that you can't hear him now?' Kars retorts.

Why does the boy think Ravian is stupid? The pirate must have seen him coming on board and quickly silenced Lasse. That must be it. And Kars is obviously in on it. He must be Pirate Bank's apprentice, a pirate in training. He looks at Kars. He doesn't really look like a pirate. Maybe that's something you learn later.

'It'd be easy enough,' says Ravian, 'to lock him away somewhere. Or to tie a handkerchief over his mouth. Or maybe you gave my dad a sleeping drug. Anything to keep him quiet, right?' He chatters on. 'Do you really think I can't find him? That I won't look everywhere? He's here. I'm sure of it. And now I'm here too. For the rest of my life! You

can't hide him from me!' He looks at the door
that leads inside the ship, but he doesn't dare to go
through it. He wants to put it off for as long as he
can. Who knows who else might have been lured on
board or is being held captive here? The men in the
pub said the pirate had lots of slaves. Now Ravian is
stuck with them for the rest of his life. Forever. Ravian's
head is spinning. Maybe the curse doesn't exist. But
maybe it does. First, he has to find Lasse. And fast.
Maybe then he can still get off the ship before they
set sail.

'Okay. I'm going to find him. Then I'll get him out
of here.' Ravian turns around and walks to the small
door. Secretly he's hoping that Kars will stop him. He's
afraid of what he'll find in there. Maybe he'll bump
straight into that pirate . . .

'Wait!' says Kars. Phew. See, he *is* hiding
something behind the door. 'I'll come with you. And
I'll get you a dry blanket. And something for that cut
on your chin.'

Ravian doesn't want to admit it, but he's happy to have Kars's help.

Kars stands up. His wet hair is stuck to his forehead.

Ravian glances up at Marvin, who's hovering above.

'Marvin, come down. You're about to blow away!'

'MEEE . . .' Marvin squeaks back from the air.

Kars glances up at the seagull, who seems exhausted.

'Marvin?' Kars says. 'Don't be scared. Seagulls don't get cursed.'

Ravian looks at him, one eyebrow raised.

'The sea doesn't curse its creatures,' Kars says solemnly.

Marvin hesitates, but then lands on a crate and gives his wings a rest.

Kars opens the door, which Ravian still hasn't dared to touch.

'Come on,' he says. 'Marvin's safe.'

Ravian follows Kars inside and looks back over his shoulder.

Marvin gives a little nod.

Inside, it's dry and warm, and it smells a bit like the pub after closing time: rum, ash, mould and stale sweat. Unwashed sailors and old fried fish. It's kind of familiar, which is nice but also very strange.

'Welcome on board,' says Kars. 'Follow me.'

They walk along a corridor with a low ceiling. Ravian can stand upright, but Kars has to duck a little. An oil lamp is hanging from a hook on the wall and swinging to and fro, making the boys' shadows move eerily around the walls. There's not much to see, just a lot of closed doors. Could Lasse be imprisoned behind one of them?

'Look,' whispers Kars, 'this is my cabin. On a ship you call a room a cabin.'

'Yes, I know that,' mutters Ravian.

Kars opens the door and goes inside.

'Are you coming? Then I can clean that cut on your chin. And if you like, I've got a towel for you too.'

Ravian looks at the end of the corridor. Lasse must be here somewhere . . . Or do they have a secret cellar, with cells or cages, where they lock up friendly sailors like his dad?

Without answering Kars, Ravian walks on, deeper into the dark corridor. He hears Kars give a deep sigh. The first door that Ravian comes to is on the right. He stops and puts his ear to the wood.

'Dad?' he whispers. 'Dad? Are you in there?'

There's no answer. Slowly, Ravian opens the door, which creaks a little. A cold breeze hits him. When he puts his head through the door, he doesn't see anything. It's dark and empty. No cage, no cell, no sailors, no dad. No one's been here for a long time.

Ravian closes the door and tries the next one. It's the same. Nothing. There are so many cabins on this ship! As he tries to open the fifth door, he realises there's no point. So many cabins, far too many for one pirate and one apprentice.

Then he hears a thumping sound coming from a cabin at the end of the corridor. That door is bigger than the others and the wooden frame has decorations. Ravian stops to listen there too. He can hear someone humming inside the cabin. For a moment, his heart leaps. But when he listens for longer, he can hear that it's the pirate's growling voice. He should run, but he's too curious. What if Lasse is behind that door? His hands sweating, he opens it and, as quiet as a mouse, he peeps through the gap. Inside, there's a light, and he can see empty bottles all over the floor, rolling back and forth with the rocking of the ship. There's a table in the middle of the room. Ravian freezes. A big man in a black coat is standing with his back to the door, leaning over the table. He seems completely absorbed in the map that's on the table. Is that Pirate Bank?

'We really should be on our way, hm . . .' The man looks up, as if he's heard something. As if he's listening closely. He slowly turns around. Ravian hides behind the door before the pirate can spot him and then runs quickly – and as quietly as he can – back along the corridor. He's looked inside all the cabins now, and he hasn't found Lasse. His dad suddenly feels much less close. Maybe Kars was right after all, and he really isn't here.

Disappointed, Ravian heads back to the deck, where Marvin is waiting for him. As Ravian walks past Kars's cabin, Kars gives him a friendly nod. He stands up and comes towards him.

'Got any secret rooms here, where you keep your prisoners?' Ravian says. But he's actually given up hope already.

'This whole ship is a prison,' Kars replies. 'There's no need to make more prisons inside it.'

Ravian nods, even though he's still not sure what to think. He walks through the door to the deck and outside.

The wind's still blowing and the rain's pouring down. Marvin is soaked and looking sorry for himself.

'Come on, Marvin,' says Ravian, picking him up and putting him on his shoulder. He's heavier than usual because of his wet feathers. 'Dad's not here. We need to be quick. They're about to leave. I think we still have time to get off the ship now. I'm sure the curse won't be a problem and if I stay on board this ship for too much longer, I'm so scared that I might faint.'

Ravian walks to the gangplank. He looks back. Kars is standing in the doorway, watching him with a bewildered expression. Then Ravian takes hold of the rail.

'Bye, then!' he calls out awkwardly to Kars, who doesn't reply.

He places his left foot on the gangplank.

See? Nothing wrong.

But when Ravian goes to put his other foot on the gangplank, he feels a huge force pushing against his leg. As if there's a wall around the ship. He tries again, but more quickly and firmly this time. Ow! He stubs his toe on the invisible wall.

'How did I bang my toe? There's nothing there!' he shouts in frustration.

He puts both feet back on board and tries it the other way around. First right, then left. And again, he's pushed back. Getting one limb off the ship – that works. But his foot, his knee, and shoulder at the same time – it doesn't work. Defeated, he turns back to Kars. He has never felt the rain hitting him so hard before. His hair blows across his face. Drops of water pour from his eyelashes and sting his eyes. His shoulders hang sadly – and so does Marvin's head.

'So, the curse is real . . .' mumbles Ravian, feeling a little ashamed. A tear rolls down his cheek. Luckily, Kars can't see it because of all the rain.

Kars doesn't say anything. He just holds out his hand.

It's cold in Kars's cabin, which has a small round window. There's nothing to see through it now, but that must be different in the daytime. The curtain has a cheerful checked pattern. Not what you'd expect from a pirate. There are two small beds in the cabin. Each has a blue-and-white striped blanket, but only one of them has been slept in.

'This is my bed,' Kars says, pointing at the one with the messy sheets and blanket. He takes a big red towel from a cupboard and hands it to Ravian.

'Dry yourself quickly or you'll catch a cold,' he says calmly.

Ravian gratefully accepts the towel. It's soft and warm.

When he's dried his hair, he sits down on the other bed and looks around, rubbing the bandage that Kars has just put on his chin. He takes off his backpack and leans it against the wall. There's a lamp in the cabin that's giving off the same eerie light as in the corridor. Marvin has sat down beside it and is spreading his feathers wide to warm up. On the wall is a big pen-and-ink drawing of a beautiful ship sailing on high waves. The artist has drawn a sort of frame of shells and curls and seaweed around the edges. It smells better inside this cabin than in the rest of the ship.

'You can have that bed, if you like,' says Kars. 'Or you can choose your own cabin, but you'll have to do some work on it, as you'll have seen for yourself. We never use the other cabins. The portholes don't close properly so there are nasty draughts, and there aren't any blankets there either.'

Ravian takes the blanket off his bed and wraps it around himself.

'No, this is fine,' he mumbles. As he looks at the drawing on the wall, he feels a lump in his throat and a sharp pain in his shoulders. Then he bursts into tears – he can't hold it in any longer. He's stuck on this stupid, cold, stinking ship forever. With that scary, growling pirate. And he'll never be able to find his dad now. And what if Lasse is back at home and all of this was for nothing? His shoulders shake. He feels so ashamed. How did it come to this? Big tears roll down his cheeks. His face is wet again.

Marvin looks up and flies over to him. He nudges Ravian's shoulder with his head.

Kars smiles at him. 'You hungry?'

For a pirate's apprentice, he's pretty okay. It seems that nice pirates do exist.

In the galley, Kars gives Ravian a big bowl of hot porridge. As he takes the first mouthful, he realises how hungry he is. For a moment, he forgets how sad he is about his dad and the throbbing cut on his chin and the ache in his stomach at the thought of what lies in store for him now. Stuck on a ship: it's his worst nightmare.

'I thought I just heard Pirate Bank say you were about to leave . . .' He pauses. 'Well, that *we* were about to leave . . .'

'Ah, yes, you could be right. But it always takes him hours to make the preparations. We often don't leave until the morning,' Kars explains.

'What does he need to prepare?'

'I don't exactly know. I'm not allowed to disturb him. But I think he's actually working up courage. It can be hard, not seeing any land for a whole month, even for a pirate. Especially for someone who can't even touch the land.'

Ravian doesn't say anything. He has so many questions about the curse that he doesn't know where to start. And he's a bit scared to hear the answers too.

'How, um . . . Why is it . . . that, erm . . .' he stammers and quickly takes another spoonful of porridge.

'The curse?' asks Kars. Ravian nods.

'That's a long story. And it's actually a secret. But fine, you're part of it now, so I'll tell you.'

Ravian looks at him eagerly.

'It all began years ago when Pirate Bank lost his own ship in a bet. And what does a pirate with no ship do?'

'Um . . . steal another one?' Ravian guesses.

'Exactly. He just captures a new one,' Kars continues. 'Pirate Bank took this ship, the *Night Raider*, around ten years ago. But sadly, you can't take a ship without violence. So, he got the crew drunk and started throwing them overboard, one by one. When the first one hit the water, the rest tried to persuade Bank to let them stay, even though they were blind drunk. They even offered to work for him. But Bank didn't want them to. He wanted to be all alone, for the rest of his life. I don't know why. He's a very gloomy man, and he's not interested in being sociable. So, he dropped them all into the water, just like that. The men couldn't fight back because they'd had so much to drink.'

'And what happened then?' Ravian is so interested in Kars's story that he's forgotten to eat.

'The sea became so angry that she cursed him and the *Night Raider*. Anyone who comes on board can never leave. That's the first rule of the curse. And there's another rule. It's a nasty one, specially to plague Bank.' Kars hesitates. 'This is what I wanted to tell you before, but I was sure you wouldn't believe me.'

'What is it?'

'When people come near the ship, they hear what they want to hear most of all. It's the sea that makes the sound. That's how she lures people on board. That way, Pirate Bank will never be alone, and that is what he really wanted. That's the biggest punishment of all.'

Ravian drops his spoon in surprise. A bit of porridge splashes onto the table.

'So . . . that was . . .' he stammers.

'Yes. The sea made the sound that you thought was your father,' says Kars.

Ravian doesn't understand. He frowns.

'But how does the sea know my dad's song?'

Kars leans towards him with a serious look on his face.

'The sea knows more than you think, Ravian.' He stares outside. For a moment he seems to be bewitched. Then he stares Ravian right in the eyes. 'The sea knows everything.'

The boys just look at each other, without saying a word. It seems to go on for hours.

Then there's a thumping and banging sound from the corridor. Kars gasps. Loud footsteps are coming closer. The growling voice sighs and groans. The wood creaks. Then the door swings open. And there he is. Tall and wide. A huge coat that Ravian would fit into four times over, and big black boots. A grumpy face covered in wrinkles. Bushy eyebrows and greasy curls down to his shoulders. In his hand, he has a half-empty bottle of rum. He takes a deep breath to say something, but then he sees Ravian. His breath catches in his throat. Ravian looks up at him, not knowing what to say.

Pirate Bank's eyes grow larger, his nostrils flare, his jaw juts forward and a big frown appears on his face. He raises the bottle. Then he roars like a wild animal and throws it with all his strength at Ravian, who puts his arms over his head and ducks. There is a deafening clatter of breaking glass.

6

KARS

'No . . . no!' groans Pirate Bank. 'He . . . you . . . not again. Enough, you salty devil, enough!'

Ravian watches from the galley as Bank paces the deck. Luckily, the bottle the pirate just threw didn't hit Ravian, but it did give him a fright. The broken glass is lying all around him. On the table, on the floor and even on his stool. He holds his head in his hands. He's sure the pirate will attack him again, maybe even in his sleep. And what if Kars isn't as nice as he seems? What if it's all just acting? And Lasse . . . Now he knows for sure that he'll never see his dad again. That this will be his end. Lured in by a trick of the sea. And with nothing in return.

'W-why did he do that?' Ravian stammers.

Kars is glaring at the pirate. He doesn't reply.

'Aaargh! What a mess . . .' wails the pirate. Then he yells in fury, 'I'll get you! Just you wait! I'll make short work of you!'

Ravian shivers. Bank's not going to leave it at throwing that one bottle at his head. He'll do whatever it takes to get rid of Ravian. It's not like he can throw him overboard, but what he *can* do might be even worse. Ravian starts panting. His hands are clammy, and he gives Kars a panicked look.

'Ravian, calm down. It's not what it seems.'

'What's do you mean?'

'He's not *really* angry.'

Ravian looks at the pirate, who is ranting and cursing. Stamping around and swinging his big arms. He grabs a lantern and throws it at the rail with all his might. It breaks and the pieces tumble overboard with a splash.

'Are you sure?'

'Yes,' Kars replies. 'Well, he *is* angry, but not with you.'

'Really?'

'Pirate Bank is a . . . complicated man. I could tell you all about it now, but you'll see for yourself soon enough. He's angry with the sea. His punishment is working well. That curse is really hurting him. And every time he's reminded of it, he explodes again.'

Ravian nods.

'But throwing that bottle at you? That was going too far.' Kars sighs. 'Just keep your head down for now. In a few days' time, he'll be calm again.'

Kars stands up and walks to the door. It's quiet on deck now. Pirate Bank has returned to his cabin.

'Come on,' says Kars. 'We'd better get out of here.'

Ravian follows Kars. He does his best to stay calm and not panic again, but it's not easy. He wants to believe Kars when he says that Bank will soon calm down, but he's not sure. He doesn't feel safe anywhere on this ship. He's never felt safe on any ship. And he certainly doesn't feel safe on this one.

They have to cross the deck to get back to the crew quarters. The storm has eased a little, but the light of the moon is still bright. Every step Ravian takes feels wobbly.

Suddenly Kars stops and holds up a finger.

'Did you hear that?'

Ravian listens. He hears the planks creaking and the waves splashing. But there's nothing out of the ordinary. Ravian walks to the rail and looks down. The waves are swirling in all directions and making different shapes. They're going round in circles, spirals and sometimes even figures of eight. He's never seen the sea like this before, so dark and mysterious. In Ravian's head and stomach, it's whirling and swirling, too. As he heads back inside, he resolves never to do anything to anger the sea.

The next day, Ravian wakes up in his bed. The sunlight is shining through the porthole and onto his face. The sky is bright blue, as if it's long forgotten about the storm. Ravian rubs his eyes and looks at the other bed. Kars isn't there. Neither is Marvin. Ravian gets out of bed and peers through the window, curious to see what the harbour will look like in daylight. But the harbour is nowhere to be seen. All around the ship, the waves are going up and down. There's no sign of the whirling and swirling he saw last night. They're sailing!

He leaves the cabin and goes in search of Kars. But before he heads out onto the deck, he pauses. Is the pirate out there? Running into him now wouldn't be a good idea.

But Kars is the only one standing on deck, with his hand above his eyes. Marvin is sitting on the rail beside him, looking in the same direction. They seem very comfortable together.

'Hey, sleepyhead!' Kars says, smiling.

Ravian still feels heavy with sleep, and he can tell from the curls hanging down over his eyes what a tangled mess his hair must be. He smiles nervously at

Kars. He quickly runs a hand through his hair, tries to rub the sleep from his eyes and goes to stand beside Kars.

'**KLOW KLOW,**' Marvin squawks happily.

'We're sailing . . .' says Ravian in a sleepy voice.

'That's right. We've been at sea for a few hours.'

Ravian looks at the horizon. There's nothing out there. No land, no animals, no other ships. Just the endless sea. Ravian hates ships, but if he's already on board one – if he really has no choice – then he can cling on to the fact that there's land somewhere, that there is something rocky and firm out there that doesn't sway and wobble around. But now he's going to be swaying forever. A dull ache nags away in his forehead.

'Where's Bank?'

'In his cabin. I think he's finally gone to sleep. He said this morning that he'd been awake all night.'

'Do you have to keep the ship sailing all by yourself?' Ravian asks. He's full of admiration, which actually feels a bit silly. Sailing a ship is probably completely normal for Kars. But can a boy really do such a difficult job?

Kars gives him a charming smile and shrugs.

'I've got you to help, haven't I?' he says, with a wink.

'But I . . .' Ravian feels his cheeks turning red. 'I . . . I don't know how to sail a ship!'

'Then I'll have to teach you!' Kars gives his shoulder a nudge and walks to the ship's wheel. 'Bank and I take it in turns: one sleeps while the other keeps the ship sailing. Unless we're anchored up, of course.'

The wheel is a big wooden one with little handles all around it. Kars seems to have everything under control. He holds his arms out wide, one hand on each side of the wheel, and looks calmly at the horizon. He looks as if nothing bad could ever happen to him.

'So, this is the ship's wheel. Want to give it a try?'

Ravian hesitates. He doesn't want to make a fool of himself. What if he's sick? What if he panics?

'What if I steer it the wrong way?' he mutters.

Kars smiles.

'See anything here that you might bump into?'

Ravian looks at Marvin, who's still sitting on the rail in the morning sunshine. He walks to the wheel and nervously takes hold of one of the little handles. He can feel how sweaty his hands are. He's terrified, but he's going to have to learn how to do it anyway. Thanks, sea. Thanks for your stupid curse.

'Look, you hold it like this.' Kars shows him and then steps back so that Ravian can take over. 'And you just steer. It's simple. If you turn it to the right, you'll sail to the right. The sails help too, but I'll teach you all about that later.'

Ravian turns the wheel a little, and to his surprise it works.

'Don't you mean "to starboard"?' he says with a grin and then sticks his tongue out at Kars. It feels so powerful to steer such a big ship with such a small movement of his hand. Ravian is starting to enjoy himself. The ship turns slowly and he watches wide-eyed as the huge ship moves through the wild water.

Because of him! He could almost forget how sick it's making him feel.

'What's all this?'

The pirate's voice booms over the ship. 'Are you letting *him* steer my *Night Raider*?' Bank looms up behind the boys. He looks just as angry as he did yesterday.

Ravian is so startled that he lets go of the wheel, and Kars quickly takes over.

'Kars! How could you? You . . . herring head!' The pirate growls and shakes his fist at the boys. Slowly he stomps towards them and stands over them with a threatening glare on his face.

Ravian steps back and automatically ducks behind Kars's broad shoulders. Now, in the daylight, Ravian can see Bank properly: every deep wrinkle, every crater in his skin and every nasty hair on his grumpy face. When he's so close that Ravian can smell the rum on his breath, Bank stops.

His nose almost in Kars's face, he says quietly, 'You know what the punishment for this would be on a normal ship, don't you?' Kars doesn't move a muscle. He doesn't even blink. 'Or do I have to show you?' Kars looks right back at him, with a frown on his face. Then Bank's gaze falls on Ravian.

'So,' he says calmly, 'you're the new recruit, are you?'

Ravian doesn't know whether he's supposed to answer or not. Recruit? Well, kind of, yes. That sounds almost as if Bank doesn't mind having Ravian on board. Ravian nods nervously. Then the pirate growls and gives Kars a filthy look.

'I bet you're glad to have some company, aren't you? A little pal?'

Kars shrugs.

'Well, why don't the two of you go and have some fun together?' says the pirate, spreading his arms. 'Scrubbing my entire ship!'

He sniggers and gives Kars a shove.

'While I correct the course that our new first mate just set. First mate? Pfft. More like "second rate"!' With a booming laugh, he takes the wheel.

Kars heads inside and goes downstairs into the hold. Ravian is frozen to the spot.

'Off you go, fishface,' growls the pirate. Ravian trots after Kars.

Ravian has never been inside the hold before. It runs the length of the ship, underneath the cabins, the galley and the deck. Ravian can see the waves through the portholes. A few hammocks hang from the beams on the ceiling. Large crates are stacked in one corner. Ravian recognises them from Deaf Diederik's harbour. A huge rope is coiled up against one of the walls. There are some barrels down there and fishing nets all over the place. On one wall, in a dark corner, there are shelves with big yellow cheeses stacked up on them, with sacks of potatoes below. Further back, Ravian sees a wheel attached to a sort of trolley with a big metal pipe on top. His eyes almost pop out of his head. A cannon!

'Do you ever use that?' he asks Kars. Kars turns around and looks at Ravian, then at the cannon and then back at Ravian again. He shrugs and walks on.

He picks up two buckets and a couple of scrubbing brushes.

'Here you go,' he says, throwing a bucket in Ravian's direction.

'How do we get water? And soap?' asks Ravian.

Kars points outside.

'Seawater?'

Kars nods.

'Salt's good for the wood.'

Ravian doubts if that's really true but there's not much other water around. Kars lowers the buckets on ropes to haul up the seawater.

'We might as well start there,' he sighs, pointing at the far corner.

As they scrub away, Kars is remarkably quiet. Ravian glances at him out of the corner of his eye. Kars's face is red, his forehead is sweaty and he keeps frowning.

Is it because of the hard work? Or is he angry with Ravian? After all, Ravian wasn't very nice to Kars at first. So, is Kars annoyed that he's there?

'Kars?' says Ravian, putting down his scrubbing brush.

Kars looks up without saying anything.

'I, um . . . I'm sorry about all the bother I caused you.'

Kars puts his brush in his bucket and sits down with his back against a crate. He smiles.

'It's okay, Rav,' he says. 'Can I call you Rav?'

'Well, actually, my dad's the only one who calls me that,' says Ravian quietly.

'Oh,' says Kars. 'Sorry. Then I won't do it.'

'No, no,' Ravian answers quickly. 'It actually feels . . . comfortable. You can call me that if you like.'

The boys grin at each other.

'Do you miss him?'

'My dad? Yes, of course I do! So much.'

'Why did he leave? And where's your mother?'

'I don't know why he left. And I don't have a mum. She went away when I was still really small. Disappeared or got lost or ran off. Doesn't matter. It's always been me and Dad. And Marvin. And my dad's away a lot, but never as long as this time. He always comes back on my birthday, and sometimes he stays for a whole month. But he usually goes back to sea before long. But this birthday he didn't come.'

'So, he's at sea?'

'Yes.' Ravian gazes at the horizon. The waves rolling up and down in front of the porthole bring back that thumping ache in his forehead. Even though he just sailed this gigantic ship, the *Night Raider*, for a moment, he's still far from being cured of his fear of boats and sailing.

'He's a fisherman. He has a beautiful boat with moss-green sails.'

'Huh? So, you're a sailor's son,' Kars exclaimed, 'and you can't sail?'

Ravian feels his face turning red and looks down at his feet.

'Um, yes, I'm . . . actually . . . pretty scared of boats and the water.'

Kars laughs out loud. It gives him dimples. Ravian is surprised Kars hadn't realised sooner that he's scared of being at sea. Maybe it's not as obvious to other people as it is to himself. After all, he's the one who feels sick and dizzy.

'Scared? What of? Not every ship has a pirate on it like Bank!'

Ravian keeps his eyes on the floor.

'Sorry,' says Kars when he sees that Ravian isn't laughing. 'But what are you frightened of?'

'I don't know,' says Ravian with a sigh. 'Whenever I stand on a wobbly boat, particularly when I look at the water, I feel like the whole world is falling away from under me. As if I'm floating in the air. Weird, huh?'

Kars thinks for a moment.

'A bit like being scared of heights?'

'Yes, I think so. But I don't have that, or at least I don't think I do. I was allowed to go all the way to the top of the lighthouse once and I wasn't scared then. So I don't know if it's the same thing.'

'My mother was scared of heights,' says Kars, 'and when she described it, it sounded a bit like what you said.'

A silence hangs over the boys for a minute, like a big raincloud.

'Where's your mother now?' Ravian asks gently. Kars looks at the floor.

'My parents are dead,' he says.

'Both of them?'

Kars nods.

Ravian bites his lip. That can always happen, too. And your mum and dad aren't away for just a while, but completely. Forever. You haven't just lost them for a time, but you'll never see them again. What should he say to Kars?

'It was a long time ago,' says Kars finally. 'They worked on a ship too. But a really big one, with about three hundred crew. My dad was a sailor, and my mum was a cook. Whenever they were at sea, I stayed with my gran. One day, the ship came back, but half of the crew had caught a disease in a far-off land.'

'Including your mum and dad?'

'Well,' says Kars sadly, 'a good friend of my dad's, who *did* come home, said my mum got sick and died not long afterwards, and that my dad died of grief.'

'Oh, that's so sad.'

'Yes, it's sad. But I was very young, and I didn't really know them all that well because I hardly ever saw them. Then, when I was almost thirteen, my gran died. That really was awful. I didn't have anyone left.' Kars tells it so easily, as if he's explaining how to butter a slice of bread.

'So, I went travelling. I don't know how long for, a few months or so. I walked a long way and ended up far from home. And one day I was walking through the dunes, and I heard a big party in the harbour. There were people singing about the delicious food on their plates, wine glasses clinking together, and happy music playing. I thought the party was on board this ship and I went on board to ask if I could join them. I was so hungry! But as soon as I set foot on the deck, the sound of the party stopped. And all I could see was a drunken pirate who'd fallen against his crates of rum.' Kars lies down on the floor, with his tongue sticking out of his mouth and his legs apart, to show the state Bank was in when he met him. Ravian bursts out laughing. A good laugh – it's just what he needs!

'So, yes,' Kars continues, 'it was a pretty big disappointment, but once Bank had got used to me, it wasn't so bad being here.'

'What do you mean? He was really horrible to you just now!'

'Yeah. He gets like that sometimes.' Kars shrugs.

'In the pub, they told me that Bank keeps slaves here and that they have to work for him,' Ravian says quietly.

Kars bursts out laughing. 'Nope, don't think so.'

'So, why haven't more people been lured on board? The sea's plan isn't working out very well, is it?'

Kars raises one eyebrow. 'Why do you think we pick up our supplies at a deserted harbour with a deaf harbourmaster?' He stands up. 'Come on, let's get back to work. We've still got loads to do.'

When they've worked their way around almost the entire hold with soapy water, scrubbed under all the hammocks, between the barrels and even behind the crates, the boys come to the last part, at the front of the ship, where the ceiling's so low that they almost bump heads. Ravian looks at Kars. He's still able to laugh, even with his sad life story. And scrub the boards as if it's no big deal. Kars looks back and gives him a puzzled smile. Ravian quickly turns his head to look at the last part of the hold.

'Do we need to go all the way back there, do you think?' He points at the huge stack of crates and boxes. They're in front of some kind of alcove.

Kars looks surprised.

'I never noticed there was anything behind those crates,' he says. 'Let's do it, just to be on the safe side.'

The boys push some boxes out of the way, so they can crawl behind them. Ravian leads the way. He scrubs really hard, because the floor here is even dirtier than the rest. When he looks up, he sees a door. It's like all the others but made of much darker wood. Half of the handle is missing. It looks like someone snapped it off.

'What . . . ? Kars, what's behind this door? Have you ever seen it before?'

Kars crawls towards him and examines the door from top to bottom. There's a big crack down the middle, as if someone once hit it with an axe. In the middle of the crack, you can see that the door isn't made entirely of wood but has a metal core.

'No . . . I've never seen it,' he says, sounding confused. He tugs at the snapped doorhandle. 'How can . . . ?'

'What?'

'That's odd. It's locked. This is the only door on the entire ship with a lock.'

7

OYSTERS

'You can go and fly with them for a bit, Marvin. As long as you come back.' Ravian is sitting beside the wheel as Kars steers. They've been sailing for three days now, three days in which Ravian hasn't seen much of the pirate.

Marvin flew over to perch on the ship's rail when he saw a group of seagulls flying by. He watches jealously as they go past.

'Go on, Marvin. You're not stuck here like we are,' says Ravian encouragingly.

Marvin glances back at him and then flies into the air to play with the other seagulls. They greet one another like old friends, even though they've never met before, and they play a game of catch with a piece of fish . . . until one of them gobbles it down.

Kars laughs as he watches the scene. Ravian closes his eyes, silently enjoying the feeling of the sun on his face. It's too cold to be on deck without a jumper, but when there's no wind, it's quite pleasant. Ravian always finds the sound of happily shrieking birds so soothing. And he knows that the pirate is fast asleep in his cabin, so there's no need to worry about him for now.

'Seagulls are very sociable birds,' he explains to Kars.

Kars nods.

'I can see that.' They're quiet again for a while, and then he says, 'Have the two of you been friends for a long time?'

'Yes,' Ravian replies. 'Eight years now.'

When the other seagulls move on, Marvin flies back to the ship and lands on Ravian's knee.

'Back so soon?' he laughs.

'KLOW KLEEOW!' Marvin looks happy.

'Do you know what, Marvin?' says Ravian. 'Maybe you could fly with a group like that for a bit. They might even take you to a place where you'll find Dad!' Ravian's eyes twinkle with hope. Marvin looks at him.

'Well, you never know,' says Kars.

'You could be our lookout!' Ravian exclaims.

Marvin puffs up his chest.

Imagine if he really found Lasse!

'Go on, Marvin, you can still catch up with them!' says Ravian. 'You know our special call. We can always find each other again.'

Marvin nods – **KROEEEEEEE KROOTKROOT KRIEE!** – and quickly flies after the group of birds.

Ravian claps his hands and waves Marvin goodbye.

'Good luck, my friend!' he calls after him.

Huffing and puffing, Pirate Bank comes onto the deck. As if the pirate has brought a cold breeze with him, Ravian's good mood blows away instantly. He freezes and looks the pirate up and down, from his long, greasy hair to his big boots. Bank is carrying two buckets, a net and a little spade on a long stick. Does he want them to do yet more scrubbing? Bank smiles at the boys and happily holds up the tools. Kars smiles back.

'Look, kids!' says Bank. He sounds so cheerful that Ravian raises his eyebrows. Isn't he supposed to be angry and drunk all the time? Is this really the scary man who threw a bottle at his head?

'You know where we'll be sailing soon, don't you?'

Kars nods excitedly. He looks as enthusiastic as Pirate Bank.

'Yes, we should be heading straight for it. Not long now.'

'Jolly good, jolly good,' the pirate says dreamily. He puts down his things, picks up a telescope and gazes into the distance.

'What are you two talking about?' Ravian whispers to Kars. 'Where are we going?'

The pirate hears him too and turns around.

'Oyster Bay!' he screams.

'What's there?' Ravian asks Kars.

'It's a magical place, Rav. You're going to love it. The water's so blue, so clear. I don't believe in fairy tales and legends, but if I came across a mythical creature there, I wouldn't be at all surprised. And there are the most delicious oysters living on the rocks, everywhere you look!'

The thought of oysters makes Ravian happy. Finally, a mystery with a happy ending instead of something like that nasty curse. Bank is just as delighted. He does a funny little dance in a circle, lifting his knees up high. Ravian doesn't know where to look. It's pretty ridiculous, a big, bad villain of the sea, with his telescope still in his hands, galumphing around like an idiot. He looks a bit like a frog. Ravian chuckles. Kars glances at him out of the corner of his eye and gives him a lopsided grin.

'Yo-hooo!' shouts Bank, sweeping his arms up and down above his head now too.

Then he realises that the boys are laughing at him.

'Yes, you go ahead!' he says. 'You'll be laughing on the other side of your faces in an hour. Because picking oysters is a horrible job! Particularly when you have to do it off the ship!' Bank picks up the stick with the spade attached and holds it over his head.

'One of you will have to knock the oysters off the rock with this, and the other one can catch them with the net. And then all the oysters you've caught have to go into the buckets. Oh, it'll be a tasty meal, boys. For once, it's our lucky day!' He rocks gently back and forth, as if he wants to do his dance again but is just managing to stop himself.

'And . . .' he continues. 'I'm the luckiest one of all! Because now you're here, little curly-noggin, I don't have to do any work! Ha! What a life.' The pirate happily chatters away to himself as he heads back inside.

What on earth was that? Ravian looks at Kars, who shakes his head and laughs.

'They say he has the devil on his shoulder,' Kars says, still laughing. 'Well, I guess that'd be bound to get a man leaping about like that.'

Ravian frowns in confusion. Is that what the sailors in the bar meant?

'Oh, you get used to him, Rav,' Kars adds. 'You get used to him.'

As Oyster Bay appears on the horizon, the ship slows down. Bank is still inside. The boys gaze at the rocks ahead, which are getting closer and closer. There's a peaceful calm, as if no one else knows about this beautiful place. The bay is a little hidden from view by the delicate wisps of pale-pink and lavender-blue mist that are drifting around the rocks. The waves break gently on the stones, making barely any sound. The sea babbles sweetly as the *Night Raider* sails towards the bay.

'Right,' says Kars, 'here we are.'

Ravian leans over the rail to see if he can see any oysters yet. He's expecting big pink pearly shells dangling in clusters in the water, but he can only see rocks.

Then Ravian hears something strange. It's as if someone is whispering among the waves. Is it the oysters? He takes another good look at the sea, which is still gently rippling. It's odd, but also nice to see the water so calm. He goes on looking at the little waves. Then he spots something briefly surfacing. And, just as quickly, it goes back down. What is it? Again, it bobs up and dives back down. Around the thing, about ten more of the same . . . things appear on the surface. Ravian blinks. Fish?

Suddenly, a wave carries them close, and he realises what they are: seahorses! A very big group of perky little creatures, perhaps a hundred of them, is swimming through the water, like a parade. One wave after another swoops them forward in graceful leaps. They swim nimbly between the rocks. Ravian smiles. Kars was right – he isn't at all surprised to see something like that in a place like this. When he looks at Kars, he sees that he's watching them too. His eyes are sparkling, and his cheeks are flushed. They look at each other and smile. Kars raises his eyebrows, as if he wants to say, 'Didn't I tell you that you'd love it?', and then he turns back to look some more. Ravian watches as the seahorses swim away. Then he hears that voice whispering again. It seems to be coming out of the faraway waves. He wonders if some other even more magical creature is about to appear. But there's no sign of any animals. Just the calmly rippling water.

Who could it be?

Is it the sea?

He can't quite hear what's being said. But when he closes his eyes and concentrates, he can almost understand the words.

Leaf . . . bright with sun . . .

And then it's just the water. How strange, thinks Ravian. He takes another good look around at the waves. This would be the perfect moment for him to see his first mermaid. Or a singing whale or a talking sea lion. But they don't exist. He frowns. A whispering sea doesn't exist either, does it? He shakes his head. They're fairy tales, stories. But he really did hear something . . .

'Will you take the net? I'll start chiselling, and I'll show you how to do it.' Kars picks up the long stick with the spade on and gives the net to Ravian. He's cast the ship's anchor in a spot with a lot of big rocks that they can easily reach. Holding the spade, he leans over the rail and starts banging the rock.

'Huh? Why are you doing that?' asks Ravian. He still can't see any of the big shells he was expecting.

'Oysters have good camouflage,' Kars explains. 'They look just like stones, but I don't fall for their tricks. I can spot them a mile away.' He goes on bashing away with the spade. 'This one's coming loose! Hold out the net! Quickly! So you can catch it when it falls.'

Ravian stands by the rail and holds his net as close as he can, but he can't reach far enough. He has to lean forward, with the whole of his upper body over the rail.

He knows he can't fall off the boat, but his hands still feel sweaty. Holding on tightly with one hand, he keeps trying. Beads of sweat run down his forehead, and the tip of his tongue pokes out of the corner of his mouth. The net is finally in the right place to catch the oyster.

Kars looks at him and puts his thumb up, with a grin on his face. Another whack – and the oyster lets go.

Plop, into the net.

'Number one!' Kars cheers.

He goes on like that, knocking loads of oysters off the rocks. Ravian catches all of them. Some are easier than others. But then the tools are kind of difficult to use.

'Hey, Kars, I've got an idea!' Without saying anything else, Ravian turns around and walks to the door of the hold. 'Come on!'

Kars watches him go, and then shrugs and follows him.

When they reach the hold, Ravian points at the portholes. They're very close to the sea, but they're just above the surface, at around the same height as the rocks. From here, the oysters are very close and much easier to pick.

'Do these open?' he asks.

'I don't actually know,' Kars replies. Then his eye falls on the cannon. There's definitely a hatch there that opens, to stick the barrel through and fire when needed.

'Here!' Carefully, he wheels the cannon away. Those things don't just fire by themselves, do they? With a worried frown, Ravian watches as Kars moves the cannon to make room for them and then opens the hatch. Ravian breathes a sigh of relief.

Kars takes the spade off the long stick and stretches his upper body through the hole.

'Wow, this is so much better!' he shouts. 'I can't believe I never thought of it before!'

Ravian smiles. It's good being able to help. But there's something strange going on too. He feels a bit peculiar. And it's not the seasickness or his fear of the ship. Now that they're back down here in the hold, he can feel the secret room tugging at him. He's so curious that it's almost as if his body is being pulled towards it. He looks at the alcove with the hidden door.

'Kars, shall we try one more time to get inside that room?' He can't take his eyes off the door. As he slowly walks towards it, he feels as if he's a piece of iron and there's a huge magnet drawing him closer. He can't help himself.

'Rav!' Kars whispers back. 'Wait for me!'

At the door, they both stop and stare again at the wooden decorations on the frame and the big crack down the middle. Kars slowly runs his hand over it, as if he's stroking a kitten, and then he shakes his head.

'I think this was Bank's doing,' he concludes.

Ravian nods. Then he takes hold of the broken handle. He pulls again to see if he can get the door to move. But nothing happens.

'I think it was him who broke the doorhandle too,' Ravian says, sounding disappointed. He's imagining all the things that could be inside the room. Maybe an old book containing the secrets of the sea. Or a big golden crown, or treasure, or a load of chocolate. That'd be good! Or a coat that makes you invisible, or a locked-up sea nymph, or maybe that singing whale. But what he really, really wants to find behind the door is Lasse.

He puts his ear to the wood.

Kars sighs and places his hand on Ravian's shoulder.

'Come on, we have to keep working,' he says.

When they're standing by the hatch again, Kars seems a bit tired of catching oysters.

'This one's really clinging on,' he complains when they're back at work and he's trying to get hold of the largest shell.

'But look.' With a big smile, Ravian points at the sky. 'I'm sure he can help us!'

Marvin comes flying up to them. He lands on the rock, braces himself on his flat feet and, in one movement, flips the oyster off the rock with his beak. Ravian catches it perfectly.

'Bravo, Marvin!' shouts Kars.

Marvin gives Ravian a good, long look, the way only a best friend can.

'Was it fun?' asks Ravian.

Marvin nods.

'Did you find Dad?'

Marvin shakes his head.

Ravian sighs. 'Well, it would have been pretty amazing if you'd found him first time.'

'Come on, let's go and show these oysters to Bank!' says Kars, picking up the buckets.

Pirate Bank has approved of the boys' haul of big oysters and told them to go and prepare them in the galley. All Kars and Ravian have to do is open the shells with a knife, because they slurp down the oysters raw, straight from the shell. Kars has shown him what to do, and now Ravian is sitting on a box, jabbing his knife into a shell. He thinks back to when he used to wash glasses at the pub. It seems like an eternity ago, but when he works it out, it is only seven days. Who would ever have thought he'd be cracking oysters open for a crazy pirate on an enormous ship? He jabs the knife into the shell again, but it won't open.

'Um . . .' He holds the shell up to Kars, who smiles.

'Okay, one more time.' Kars comes and stands beside Ravian and holds his hand with the knife in it.

'Look, like this. There you go!' says Kars, making exactly the right movement with Ravian's hand in his. 'It's in the wrist action.'

Ravian nods and smiles. Then he pulls the two halves of the shell apart and sees the yucky, slippery, slimy thing inside. It's about the size of a pear drop, but it looks like a big boogery blob.

'Yuck, disgusting,' he says, pulling a face. He gives the shell a shake, making the blob slip and slide around. Then he spots something gleaming at the edge of the shell. It's a little ball – and it's so stunningly beautiful that he gasps out loud.

'Wow,' he whispers. 'Kars, look.' And he holds the shell up to Kars, whose eyes light up too.

'A pearl . . .' he gasps. 'Wow . . .' Kars reaches for the shell and takes it so that he can study the enchanting ball more closely.

'I've never found one,' he says, holding the shell up close to his face with one eye shut. 'I think you bring good luck, Rav.'

Ravian feels a warm glow. Giving Kars a big grin, he takes back the shell.

Outside the galley, the planks creak, and the boys hear heavy footsteps stamping across the deck.

It's Pirate Bank.

'How's it going with those oysters?' roars Bank, swinging open the door to the galley. Ravian quickly tries to hide the oyster with the pearl. He clasps his fist tightly around it, puts both hands behind his back and sits up very straight with an innocent expression on his face. But that only attracts Bank's attention.

'What have you got there?' the pirate asks suspiciously. 'Show me!'

Ravian holds his hands tightly clasped around the shell.

'SHOW ME!'

8

THE RIDDLE OF THE SEA

With a powerful tug, Pirate Bank yanks the shell from Ravian's hands. Ravian tries to pull it back, but the pirate is much stronger. Curiously, Bank separates the two halves of the shell.

'Yes! This one's mine!' he cries triumphantly, his fat fingers plucking out the pearl. He tosses the two half-shells onto the table.

'But . . .' Ravian begins to stammer.

'What?' Bank replies threateningly. His shadow falls over Ravian as he stands next to him with his legs wide apart. 'But what?'

'Um . . . nothing. Nothing at all,' says Ravian quietly. He doesn't want to make the pirate even angrier.

'Thought not. Can we eat yet?' The pirate takes an opened oyster and slurps down the slimy gloop in one go. The corners of his mouth twitch and he closes his eyes. Then he gives a big grin and licks his lips. 'Excellent!'

That night Ravian awakes with a start. The door of the cabin squeaks. There are footsteps in the doorway. He freezes and doesn't dare to look to see if Kars is still in bed. Is the pirate coming into the cabin? But why? What's he doing? Ravian holds his breath. Footsteps quietly approach his bed. He squeezes his eyes shut. Then someone taps him on the shoulder.

'Rav. Rav, wake up!' It's just Kars. Phew. He has a lantern in his hand. Gently, he gives Ravian a shake.

Ravian sits up and leans on one arm.

'What's wrong? Is everything okay?'

Kars frowns and looks nervously at the door. Then he holds his hand in front of Ravian's face. When he opens it, the big round gleaming pearl is lying on the palm.

'Hey? How did you get hold of that?' Ravian exclaims.

'Ssh! I stole it,' says Kars with a grin. 'Well, I actually just took it back. I didn't really steal it. He stole it from *us*! It was *our* treasure.' Ravian nods. That's true.

'Yes, a special find like that should definitely stay with us,' he says.

Kars smiles at him and holds the pearl out to Ravian.

'Here, for you, Rav.'

Ravian looks at Kars in surprise. He doesn't take the pearl.

'No, no! It's *ours*!'

'From me, to you.' Kars gives him a little squeeze as he presses the pearl into his hand.

'But won't Bank be angry when he finds out?'

Kars chuckles.

'Marvin and I have already come up with a solution! He found a shiny little shell and I slipped it into the pot where Bank was keeping the pearl. That old drunkard won't even notice the difference.'

A bit later, when Kars has fallen asleep, Ravian is still awake, rolling the pearl from one hand into the other. The little round marvel that Kars let him have, just like that. Even though he thought it was really amazing, too! How much is a pearl like this worth? Must be a lot. But Ravian would never sell it. He'd rather keep it as a reminder of his adventure at sea.

That's if he ever gets off this cursed ship.

He puts the pearl safely under his pillow and falls asleep with a big smile on his face.

'What are we going to do with all this mess? Throw it overboard?' asks Ravian. It's early in the morning of his fifth day on board, and the whole deck is still covered with empty shells from the oyster feast.

'Yes, or how about stringing them together to make a necklace?' laughs Kars.

Ravian picks up a shell.

'My dad always used to put shells up to his ear. He said he could hear the sea,' he tells Kars. 'He used to do it whenever he was missing the ocean.'

Ravian holds the shell to his ear. It actually makes no sense, because he's already in the middle of the ocean. All he can hear is the horrible sea. But he tries again anyway. He closes his eyes and listens. He hears a murmur, he hears the waves, and then . . . a voice? Whispering.

Leaf in the wind . . . shhhhh shhhh
Top bright with sun . . .
Haul it in, guard it well . . .
And wait till you've won . . . shhhhhh shhhh

He opens his eyes and looks straight at Kars, who gives him a lopsided smile and wrinkles his forehead. Ravian doesn't have to say anything or to ask anything. Kars knows what he just heard.

'It's the sea,' Kars explains simply. So it's true. Was the man with the scar right about everything? But how is it possible? Ravian holds the shell to his ear again. Now he can't hear anything, just the sound of the sea as usual. Confused, he tries again and again. Was it really the sea? Or did he just think it was?

'Come and help me clear up the mess,' says Kars.

Ravian just looks again at the shell in his hand.

'That's the sea? What do you mean? The sea can't talk . . .'

Without answering, Kars picks up a shell and throws it overboard.

Is Ravian really that much of an ignoramus? What does Kars know about the sea that he doesn't?

'Does . . . she do that often?' he asks finally.

Kars looks at him and nods.

'Yes, she's always coming up with new riddles. Some of them she repeats for years, others for not so long. Maybe those are the ones that have been solved – who knows?'

'So, what she whispers isn't necessarily meant for the person who's listening?'

'No, everyone at sea hears the same riddles. That's why I don't take them too seriously.'

'It doesn't have anything to do with the curse, then?'

Kars shakes his head and shrugs. 'I don't think so. At least not to do with the *Night Raider*'s curse. I think. Like I said, the sea is a riddle to everyone.'

Ravian holds the shell to his ear again. But the voice of the sea is still silent.

'But what does it all mean?'

'Well, if I knew that . . .' Kars throws another shell over the rail. 'You should ask Bank about it. It sometimes really riles him up.'

'So, does he know what it means?'

'No,' replies Kars, 'that's why it drives him so crazy! Are you going to help me clear up?'

Ravian sighs.

From the deck, they throw the shells into the sea, one by one. They make a game of it, to see who's best at throwing. Splash, splash. Splash, splish. Splosh, **BONK!**

'What was that?' asks Ravian in surprise. Kars just shrugs.

Ravian screws up his eyes to take a better look. A head pops up out of the water, right where the shell just landed so hard. A small, greenish head. Then it goes back down. And pops back up again. It looks their way. And then a big, shiny shell comes floating to the surface.

'Kars!' Ravian points at the water.

Kars narrows his eyes too.

'A turtle! But what's up with her?' he says.

'What do you mean?'

'There's something wrapped around her shell. Looks like she's stuck in something.'

The turtle slowly comes closer to the ship.

'It's rope!' shouts Ravian. 'She's trapped in a tangle of rope! Poor thing!' It's as if some bad guy tied her up and she's just managed to escape. It wouldn't surprise Ravian if this is the sea's fault as well.

'We have to help her,' says Kars.

Marvin flies over to the turtle and squawks something at her. He stays near the turtle as she swims to the ship. When she's close enough, Ravian grabs the net he was using to catch the oysters, and then he fishes her out of the water in one smooth movement.

'Come on, little turtle,' he says in a soothing voice, 'we're going to help you.'

Carefully, Kars takes her from the net and puts her on the deck. He kneels beside her. She looks up at him with her little black beady eyes.

'Ssh . . . stay calm,' he whispers. 'We're not going to hurt you.' He holds out his hand and gently strokes her head. She withdraws into her shell a little.

'How did you get all tangled up like this, girl?' Kars starts pulling the ropes apart. Ravian watches calmly.

What a beautiful animal she is, this turtle. With funny skin, like a little old granny.

'There you go . . .' says Kars, carefully untangling the long pieces of rope. 'Nearly done.'

'Do you think turtles give each other names?' asks Ravian, gently stroking her flipper. 'Or don't you have a name?' He looks at Kars and smiles. Kars smiles back.

'I'm going to call you Sol,' says Ravian finally.

'Yes, that's a nice name,' says Kars. 'There you go, Sol. You're free!'

Sol moves forward a little, but it looks painful. She makes a groaning sound.

'Ah, no, look. She's hurt! The rope's cut her,' says Kars.

'It wasn't that shell we threw, was it?' Ravian asks in a worried voice. He'd never be able to forgive himself for hurting her.

Kars shakes his head. 'No, you heard the loud noise the shell made, didn't you? It hit her on the back.

That wouldn't have hurt her. And the wound is right where the rope was, you see?'

'We need to keep her with us for a while,' says Ravian. 'Then we can take good care of her until she goes back into the sea. Does that sound good, Sol?' She blinks, as if she wants to say that it sounds very good.

'Aha! I see you've already caught dinner for this evening!' Pirate Bank suddenly bellows. 'Turtle soup! My favourite!'

He stomps in his big boots towards the boys and the turtle – and pulls a knife out of his belt.

'Give that creature to me. I'll take it from here!'

9

MARVIN

The pirate's shadow falls over the boys and Sol the turtle as he comes closer.

KLINGKLINGKLANG . . . KLINGKLING . . . **BANG!**

Bank spins around.

'What's going on over there?' he yells. In one corner of the deck, where there are a few half-empty bottles of rum, Marvin is wildly flapping around. A bottle falls and rolls away and another one smashes on the floor.

'You flying rat!' shouts Bank, waving his knife at Marvin, who flies off and perches high up in a mast.

'I'll make seagull steaks out of you!' Bank yells up at him. Ravian seizes his chance and hurries inside, hugging Sol to his chest. Then Bank turns around.

'Where's that blasted turtle gone?'

Kars peers around. He searches the deck and even looks over the rail.

'Huh? How did that happen?' he says, pretending to be surprised. 'Well, um . . . No idea. I think it must have slipped off the ship. It's escaped!'

He clenches his fist to show the pirate how annoyed he is.

'Amateur!' hisses Bank. He puts away his knife and, with a deep sigh, walks off.

In one of the cabins where no one ever goes, Ravian has put a pillow on a bed for Sol and wrapped her in a blue-and-white striped blanket, which he ran to fetch from his own cabin.

'We'll make sure he doesn't find you, Sol,' he whispers.

* * *

When Ravian goes back onto the deck, Marvin is still sitting up on the mast.

'Thanks, Marvin!' shouts Ravian. 'That was a good distraction.'

Marvin flies in a circle around Ravian. When he lands on his shoulder, they gaze together at the horizon.

It's so far away. And there's so much sea. And the sea they can see now is just a small part of it all. Beneath the surface and beneath the waves, there's a hundred times as much sea. The sky looks almost the same colour. Everything is blue, but also a little grey. Ravian feels incredibly small as he looks out at that endless mass of water. He's surprised that the sea seems to be bothered about something as little as one bad pirate. Why should the sea care what one person does? Is that how she keeps everyone in her power? All the creatures who live in her? And the villains who sail on her? The man with the scar said the sea sends sailors on strange courses. Is that what happened to Lasse? Ravian frowns and worries that the sea might know everything about him too. Not that he has any really bad secrets. One time he stole a cigarette and smoked it, but he thought it was disgusting. And it's also a bit of a secret that he's scared of ships. He'd rather not talk about it at any rate. And now he's a sailor on a cursed ship . . .

A sailor. Ravian smiles at the horizon. His dad will be so proud when he hears that.

A black cloud appears in the distance. It's moving, and it seems to be getting bigger and bigger. Marvin and Ravian stand and watch. It doesn't look like there's a storm on the way, and it doesn't feel very threatening. But what could it be?

'**KLOW KLOW KLOW!**' Marvin cries, flying up into the air. And then Ravian sees it too. It's the group of seagulls Marvin played with when they'd only just joined the *Night Raider*.

'Are you going to go off with them again?' Ravian asks hopefully. 'Are you going to look for Dad?'

Marvin shrieks and nods. He lands on Ravian's head for a moment and gently stamps. Ravian laughs. When the seagulls are almost at the ship, Marvin flies off. The birds shriek happily at one another, and Marvin flies along with them.

'Good luck, gulls!' Ravian shouts after them. He gives a deep sigh as he watches his best friend flying away. When will they see each other again? He hopes he hasn't lost both his dad and his friend.

The seagulls aren't big talkers. The bird that's flying at the front is a bit grumpy and, with his tattered grey feathers, he's clearly the oldest. The group flies silently at top speed, with a clear destination in mind. Marvin doesn't know where they're going. He is at the back of the group. The seagull beside him gives him a friendly nod when he catches his eye.

After two days of flying in silence, there's still no sign of land, and Marvin hasn't seen any ships other than the *Night Raider*. The group of seagulls occasionally stopped to rest on pieces of driftwood or on a rock sticking out of the water. Some of the water they flew over was rough, and Marvin saw orange and purple sparks in the waves, whirling and swirling around. He would have liked to stop to take a look, but the group kept on flying and it might have been dangerous to get too close, so he always flew on quickly.

Marvin knows only too well how wildly the sea can behave. He's seen it all: how she roughs up sailors, how she floods entire cities and snaps boats in two as if they are matches. But also how she is like a soft satin gown for her fish and her lobsters and monsters that live on the bottom, completely in the dark. So he can't hate her. He knows that the sea does what she thinks is best.

Marvin is pretty tired now. Maybe it's time to go back. After all, he's been flying for two days. The sun is low, so they must have been flying for a few hours. And if he goes too much further, he won't be able to find the *Night Raider* again. If only he could land somewhere to rest. Should he go back? He'd be better off staying with the other seagulls. On his own, he would feel so lonely and such a long way from home. The rest will be getting tired soon, won't they?

Marvin quietly hums Lasse's adventuring song, which distracts him. He forgets the pain in his wings, he forgets his fear of not being able to find Ravian, and he forgets how endless his journey seems. The gentle sea breeze blowing through the feathers on his head is nice and cool. The birds around him know what they're doing. He can do this. He has to. And then, after the third verse, a small island appears in the distance.

On the island, there are tall trees with huge green leaves and fruits in their crowns. Marvin lands in the top of the first tree he sees. The rest of the group flies on, but Marvin has had enough. He can feel his heart pounding in his wings. The sun is setting, turning the island a beautiful orange red. Marvin decides to spend the night here and to go in search of the *Night Raider* tomorrow.

He looks down from the tree. There's a campfire on the beach and he can hear music. It's not the kind of music that Marvin is used to. It's nothing like the sea shanties that the people in the pub at the harbour always sing. Someone's banging a big drum, and there are instruments with bells and shells on them. He also sees a flute made of reed. People are screaming and whooping and dancing barefoot in circles around the fire. There's just one man who isn't dancing. He's sitting with his eyes closed and shouting up at the sky. Marvin doesn't know what's going on. He's never seen anyone do that before.

When Marvin looks the other way through the trees, he sees a clearing where a group of people is sitting. One of them keeps pointing at someone, then throwing dice and babbling strange words that Marvin doesn't understand.

The people all look strange. Different. They have pictures on their faces and beads in their hair. The clothes they're wearing are brightly coloured – purple, pink and blue – and big and loose and threadbare. Marvin's never seen anyone like them in Rottenherring.

'Please, oracle! Tell me!' someone shouts, at the foot of Marvin's tree. Marvin peers down through the leaves. More strange people. Each one seems stranger than the last.

'Lady Venus, please tell me how . . .' The man beneath the tree is kneeling in the sand with his hands together, and he doesn't finish his sentence. He has a blue-and-white striped blanket tied around his shoulders and a hat on his head. Around his neck is a chain with a big pomegranate on it.

Across from him, a woman in an almost see-through pale-pink gown is sitting in an enormous shell. She has very long orange-brown hair, which is blowing gently in the wind.

'Ssh . . .' she says soothingly to the man. She holds a shell to her ear. 'If you keep wailing and begging like that, I can't hear it, and then I can't help you.'

'Sorry, my lady,' the man says. 'Forgive me.'

The woman sits quietly for a while, with the shell up to her ear. She listens closely.

'The curse of the quail's sermon . . .' She opens her eyes. 'Ever heard of that one?'

The man shakes his head.

'No. Could that be it?' he asks anxiously. The woman listens again to the shell and doubtfully twitches her mouth to one side.

'The sufferer has nightmares . . . about people being burned at the stake and about frogs raining from the sky . . . All sorts of nasty scenes like that. But –' she takes a good look at the man – 'then your tongue would also have turned into a twig. I don't think that's the case, is it?'

The man touches his tongue.

'No, it's still made of tongue.'

The woman closes her eyes again. The man nervously rocks back and forth.

'The curse of Orsobuko,' she says finally. 'With that one, the dreams are all in black and white.

And . . . it always ends with the dreamer being eaten by a bear. The curse of Orsobuko can be lifted by not eating a single piece of meat during the lifetime of one bear.' She opens her eyes and looks questioningly at the man. 'Does that sound familiar?'

'No, no, my lady. I've already explained to you, haven't I?' wails the man. 'A figure, a shadow of a man. Right next to my bed. And then that pressure! That pressure on my chest. Oh, oh, my lady. My night rest has been stolen from me. I want to sleep normally again! Even if it's only for one night!'

The woman sighs and looks away. She's got it wrong twice now.

'Now listen, sir. I'm an oracle, not a doctor,' she snaps. 'I can communicate with the sea and ask her all about the curses she has uttered, but I don't have any sleeping pills for you.'

'Oh, Lady Venus, forgive me. I know I shouldn't be bothering you, but I have no other choice! You're my last option. If you can't help, I'll walk into the sea myself until I can hear her and she finally puts me out of my misery.' The man starts crying now and falls forward. With his face in the sand and his hands on the woman's feet, he sobs and sobs.

'Please, please!'

'Go on, then. I'll try it one more time.' She kicks his hands off her feet. 'Let's see. A man beside your bed, you say . . .' She closes her eyes. She whispers and mumbles. 'In the night . . . night rest . . . the curse of the *Night Raider*?' She opens her eyes for a moment, but then closes them again to listen. 'With that curse, um . . .' She frowns.

Marvin listens closely. It can't be a coincidence.

Then Lady Venus shakes her head.

'Oh no, no. This is something else,' she says.

'What is it? What are you keeping from me? The curse of the *Night Raider* sounds like it could be the right one, noble lady. The *Night Raider* must be that spirit, yes, the man who stands by my bedside and presses me into my mattress when I try to get up, yes, yes . . .'

'No, my good man, this is a curse related to a very old ship. Once you've set foot on it, you can never leave.'

The man falls silent.

'There is a scary figure on the ship, though,' Lady Venus continues, 'the one the curse began with, but I'm sure it's not the same man as in your dreams. Because he is trapped there, along with his soul. And he'll probably never have his curse lifted, because that would mean risking his life for someone else. And there's no way that villain will ever do that. At least, that's what the sea tells me.' Lady Venus puts the shell down beside her and stands up. 'Right, it's my break now. Come back later.'

Marvin is left behind in his treetop, beak wide open in surprise.

Meanwhile it's got dark and more people have come to dance around the fire. They're having fun and making lots of noise. Marvin flies up to take a better look at them. They act so differently from the folk in

Rottenherring. When he lands on the sand by the fire, a little girl with big blue eyes walks over to him.

She holds out her hand and strokes his head with her finger.

'Shaa-reh!' she says to him and then she walks away, back to her father by the fire.

Marvin makes a snug hollow in the sand. When he closes his eyes, he imagines that he's home and sleeping in the dunes by the house, as Ravian and he sometimes do when it's hot in the summer. With the heat of the fire, the music and the tiredness in his wings, he quickly falls asleep.

After Marvin wakes up the next day, he goes for a little walk in the sea. He pecks a small crab out from under a stone for his breakfast, he digs his feet into the wet sand until he can't see them any more, and he builds a tower of shells. Then he decides that it's time to go in search of the *Night Raider*. He has an important job to do now. He flies up a long way to see if he recognises anything out there in the distance.

And while he's high up there in the air, he glances back down . . . and sees the best thing he could have wished for.

10

THE STING

Ravian wonders how long they've been sailing for. Two weeks? He's sitting on the edge of the *Night Raider*'s deck, with his legs dangling through the railing above the water. Kars suggested that he should do it every day, to get over his fear. For the first few days, Ravian didn't dare, even though he knows he can't fall off the ship and into the water – because of the curse. It's going pretty well, although he still doesn't like looking down. Kars keeps reminding him that there's nothing scary about it: falling overboard is impossible. And although that hasn't made his fear go away completely, it helped a bit.

Ravian kicks his heels against the side of the ship. How is Lasse doing? Is his boat damaged? Has he run aground on the wild white cliffs? Are the boat's moss-green sails torn to shreds and drooping over the ship like weeping willows? Or is he maybe lost? Has his rudder snapped off and is he drifting in an unknown direction? On an endless route without a destination? Or is he stranded somewhere, and has he fallen in love with a nymph or a mermaid? And has that made him forget Ravian? Or even worse, could he be . . . Ravian shakes his head. Don't think about that.

'Hi,' says Kars, coming to sit beside him.

Ravian nods. 'Hi,' he mumbles.

'Everything okay?'

Ravian shrugs. 'I was just thinking about my dad.'

Kars gives a serious nod.

For a while, they sit together in silence, with their legs dangling overboard. Half captive, half free.

'Kars?'

'Yes?'

'Do you think the riddle has something to do with that secret room?'

Now it's Kars's turn to shrug. He gazes into the distance, narrowing his eyes to keep out the sun.

'No idea, Rav,' he says calmly.

Ravian has so many questions, but he doesn't dare to ask them all. He doesn't want to drive Kars crazy, and anyway he usually gets a shrug of the shoulders in response. If there's a riddle, there must be an answer too, mustn't there? A solution? But what would it solve? And what's in that room? And why isn't Kars more curious? It's hardly surprising that Ravian gets stomach-ache when he thinks about the sea. And that he can't imagine anything more terrible than tumbling down into the sea and being swallowed by all of that immense blue. Everyone's afraid of the sea and her dangers.

So he just says, 'What are we going to do today?'

'Um, catch shrimp, I think. How does that sound?' says Kars.

'Yeah, fun.' Ravian tries to sound casual. But then a sigh slips out. 'I've never done it before, though. How do you do it?'

'With a net.' Kars points at a mast with a big net hanging on it. 'We're sailing into an area where there are lots of shrimp, and then we'll get to work.'

'You know so much stuff,' says Ravian, sighing again and then smiling at Kars.

Kars gives him his lopsided grin.

'Yes, I've been travelling this exact same route for more than a year. So now I know it by heart.'

'Why do you never sail a different way?'

'I once suggested that to Bank, but he's scared to death of missing his rum supplies at Deaf Diederik's harbour.'

Ravian laughs. Of course – that would be a disaster for Bank. More questions come rising up inside him like bubbles in beer.

'So, why do you only ever moor at full moon?' he asks.

Kars chuckles.

'There's an old sailing superstition that you shouldn't moor at full moon. I think it has something to do with evil spirits, which roam the land when the moon is full and could come on board. It's nonsense if you ask me. But for Bank, it's because it means there won't be many people in the harbour then. And obviously he doesn't want any more people on his ship.' Kars chuckles again. 'You were the only evil spirit to come on board this time.' He gives Ravian a gentle thump on the arm. 'And I think that's –' he smiles – '. . . a very good thing indeed.'

At the end of the afternoon, the boys hang the net out. Pirate Bank helps them to prepare. He doesn't say a word to them. He's not angry and he's not oddly cheerful, he's not acting strangely at all. He's just quiet. Ravian watches him out of the corner of his eye. He's beginning to get used to Bank and realising that he's not as scary as the men in the pub said. But Bank does have unpredictable moods. Maybe another unexpected side of him will emerge.

When the net's in place, Kars carefully lowers it into the sea with a rope that goes through a hook on a beam.

'When do we haul it back up?' asks Ravian.

The pirate sighs impatiently.

'In about half an hour. But when the net gets heavy, it'll start pulling on the beam. So we'll be able to see when it's time to bring it up,' Kars explains.

Bank walks away and lies down on an old crate. Ravian watches the net in fascination.

'How's Sol doing?' asks Kars.

'Shsh!' Ravian hisses back. He nods in the pirate's direction. 'He'll hear you!'

Kars looks at him apologetically.

'I'm going to go and check on her,' he whispers, disappearing inside.

A few minutes later, he comes back, holding the pillowcase that Sol was sleeping on. There are a few bloodstains on it.

'We need to keep an eye on her, eh?'

Ravian feels a lump in his throat when he sees the blood. Poor Sol. He nods, with a serious expression.

'What are you two whispering about over there?' the pirate asks suspiciously. Oh, he's back to his old self, thinks Ravian. The grumpy captain has returned. But then the pirate sighs and dramatically throws one hand in the air.

'Ah, I'm not interested anyway. Forget about it.' He turns over and falls into a deep, snoring sleep. The boys look at each other and try not to laugh.

Then the beam begins to creak. That means the net must be getting nice and full of shrimp.

'Look!' says Ravian.

Kars has already noticed too, and he starts hauling up the net.

'Bank, wake up!' he says.

Ravian is surprised that Kars dares to speak to him like that. Did Kars and Bank sometimes used to have a good time when it was just the two of them travelling together? Did they even become friends? That's hard

164

to imagine, but they must know each other quite well by now.

Kars shouts over to Bank again. 'Hurry up, pirate! I need you over here.'

'You've got that lad to help you now,' Bank replies sleepily, turning to look at the boys.

'We need you too. It's a heavy load!' shouts Kars, but the pirate just lies there. So Ravian and Kars tug at the rope together until the net rises a bit out of the water.

'Hey! Come and help!' shouts Kars. 'It's never been this heavy before!'

'Okay, okay, I'm coming,' mutters Bank, trudging over to the boys. 'I can't leave anything to you, can I, you little sea slug?!'

The three of them pull at the ropes. When they've lifted the net all the way out of the water, they turn the beam, so that their catch is dangling over the deck.

Ravian gasps. 'Hey, what *is* that?' But Kars has already let go of the ropes. Thud. The net falls onto the deck with a dull sound.

There are no tasty pink shrimp in the net. Nope.

What's in the net is blubbery and squidgy and slippery.

Jellyfish!

Their creepy tentacles are entangled in the net.

Kars looks shocked and shakes his head.

Pirate Bank rubs his eyes. 'Oh, lads! Oh no . . .' he mumbles, walking over to the rail. He looks into the waves. 'Jellyfish . . . that is . . . that means . . . Oh no, lads, shivering sea otters!'

Ravian stares at the slimy jellyfish. A few have tumbled out of the net while they were hauling them in. What's the problem? They can just throw them back into the sea, can't they? What's all the panic about? Maybe he should try to keep a jellyfish for Sol. Lasse once taught him that turtles sometimes eat jellyfish. But how would you go about picking up one of those things? And, more important, how is he going to take it to Sol without Bank noticing?

Pirate Bank is still wailing away and staring at the waves of wobbly jelly. Then he stomps back towards his cabin, right past a jellyfish that has escaped from the net.

'OW!' he yells. 'OW OW OW!'

'He's been stung!' Kars shouts. He runs over to the pirate. Bank has fallen to the deck. Glistening beads of sweat are running down his forehead and cheeks to his chin.

'Blasted beasts and their stings!' he curses.

'Let me take a look,' says Kars. 'Keep calm.'

Pirate Bank's leg is turning red and coming out in blisters, and – worse than that – there's still a bit of tentacle stuck to his skin!

'OW!' he screams again. 'Get it off me, Kars, get it off!'

Kars grabs a bucket of water from the galley and gently wrings out a sponge over the red leg. Ravian stands there, feeling helpless. He wants to help, but he doesn't know how. Kars seems to have a solution for everything. He's just like Lasse.

'Aaargh! Stop it! You're making it worse!' shouts Bank.

Kars looks at Ravian.

'What now?' They both look around. Then Ravian runs to the galley too. A plan is emerging from the mist inside his head. Bit by bit. Maybe it's a stupid idea, but he has to do something. Kars and Bank need him. He grabs a bottle of rum from the cupboard and hurries back.

'Maybe this will help!'

He takes the cork from the bottle and splashes some rum over the tentacle on Bank's leg. The pirate groans. Nothing will help the pain. But the tentacle reacts to the alcohol. It shrivels, turns pale and then lets go, falling defeated to the ground. That seems to calm the pirate for a moment, but then the pain of the blisters hits him and he starts screaming again.

This is Ravian's chance.

The pirate isn't really aware of what's going on now, anyway. Ravian throws another big splash of rum over the jellyfish that stung Bank. The jellyfish shrivels and shrinks. Ravian grabs a stick and stabs the dead jellyfish, like a knight heroically plunging his sword into a dragon to save the princess. But it's a dragon made of jelly and the princess has a green shell. Ravian chuckles and heads to Sol's cabin, holding the skewered jellyfish in front of him.

'I don't know what else we can try,' Kars whispers to Bank. He says it as gently as possible, hoping to calm the pirate. He looks over his shoulder, but there's no sign of Ravian. 'Rav?'

Then Ravian returns with a little bottle in his hand. The pirate's almost crying now because he's in so much pain.

'Look, this stuff will help.' He shows them the bottle. 'Captain, this will ease your pain. But first it's going to sting even more for a little bit. Okay?'

Bank nods. There's nothing left of that crazy old captain and his bellowing. Ravian opens the bottle and empties it over the blisters.

'Aaargh!' Bank roars, but he calms down after a minute or two.

'Is that better, captain?' Ravian asks quietly.

'Yes, I think so,' he says with relief. 'But please, lad, just call me Bank, eh?'

Ravian nods happily. Kars looks at him with a puzzled expression, but Ravian doesn't say anything.

When the boys are lying in bed that night, Kars is still curious.

'So, where did you get that miracle medicine?'

Ravian smiles mysteriously.

'Oh, go on. Tell me!' Kars insists.

'My dad once told me about jellyfish stings . . . and how to clean them. And, um, well . . .' Ravian can't hold in his laughter any longer. 'You have to use pee!'

Kars looks surprised.

'You peed in that bottle?'

Ravian bursts out laughing.

'Yes!' he cries. 'I obviously didn't dare just to pee on the pirate. I'm not an idiot!'

Kars is roaring with laughter now too.

'Wow! You peed on Bank!'

11

SWIMMING IN ICE CREAM

Pirate Bank limps across the deck on his swollen leg. It's early in the morning and it looks like it's going to be a cloudy day. It was yesterday when they caught the jellyfish, but the *Night Raider* is still surrounded by the blubbery beasts. Ravian is standing by the mast because he's recently discovered that it's where he feels the rocking of the ship the least. He stares at the pirate. The pirate stares at the sea, making the occasional growling sound. He doesn't really sound angry, more like worried. Is Kars still sleeping? When Ravian got up he looked across at Kars's bed and saw him lying in a funny position, with his legs curled up beneath him. Ravian chuckles at the thought.

'Kars,' says Bank to Ravian.

Kars . . . Kars?

Ravian is startled out of his daydream and blushes, as if Bank just read his mind.

'Where's Kars?'

Oh.

'He's still asleep, captain. I mean, um . . . Bank. Mr Pirate. Bank, sir.'

The pirate looks at him with a raised eyebrow, then shakes his head and turns back to the sea. Ravian could kick himself. Nice one, Ravian. That was really cool and tough.

'Could I help?'

'Hmpf,' mutters Bank.

'Have I done something wrong?'

The pirate doesn't reply but goes on anxiously limping back and forth. He leans over the rail and stares down at the waves. Then he walks to the other side of the ship and does the same. And back again.

'What's up with him?'

Startled again, Ravian sees Kars standing beside him.

'Hey, where did you appear from?'

Kars leans his arm on Ravian's shoulder. It feels good.

'The real question is: what are you doing up so early?'

'Big waves,' says Ravian. 'Couldn't sleep.'

Kars nods. He frowns at the pirate, who's so busy looking at waves and limping to and fro that he hasn't even noticed Kars.

'And I don't know what's up with him,' says Ravian, 'but he asked for you.'

Kars walks over to Bank.

'Hey! What's going on? You need to sit down, pirate. All that walking's no good for your jellyfish sting!'

'Yeah, yeah, I know . . .' Bank replies, but he goes on pacing. 'But that's exactly the problem!'

'What?'

'Those jellyfish!'

'We washed them all overboard, Bank. They're safely back in the sea.'

'Blasted barnacles!' curses Bank, shaking his head. 'You just don't get it, do you?'

He limps over to the rail on the port side, leaving the confused boys behind.

'I just went to see Sol, to check how she's doing,' says Kars quietly when he's back beside the mast with Ravian.

'And?'

'Pretty well, I think. Her wound's almost healed. And you gave her that jellyfish, didn't you?'

Ravian nods.

'She's really perked up. That was such a great idea, Rav.'

Ravian's heart leaps.

'Can we release her soon, then?'

Kars looks over at the panicky pirate and sighs.

'Yes, I think we probably should.' He nods meaningfully in Bank's direction and grins.

Bank hobbles back towards them. He glares at Ravian. Then he walks on, grabs a big stick, lowers one end of it into the water and stirs it around.

Ravian shrugs and taps his temple with his finger. Bank suddenly turns around. 'What are you two standing around for?' he snarls.

'Um . . . we'd be happy to help,' Kars begins cautiously, 'but you need to explain what we're doing.'

The pirate looks in amazement at Kars, then Ravian and back at Kars.

'Don't you have the feeling: "Hey, this place is feeling pretty dangerous"?'

The boys look at each other and then shake their heads at the same time. Ravian always thinks it's dangerous at sea, but that's probably not what the pirate means.

'You're not thinking: "Hmm, that was a bit strange, all those jellyfish"?'

The boys shake their heads again.

'It's just one of those things, isn't it?' says Ravian. 'At home we sometimes get loads of jellyfish washing up on the beach. No one seems to think it's strange.'

'At home!' shrieks the pirate. 'No, nothing strange ever happens at home. Because everyone looks away when something's different from usual. But home –' he's so angry that he clenches his jaw as he speaks – '. . . is not here.'

Ravian can't nod quickly enough.

'Well, you'll just have to wait and see for yourselves,' says Bank, and he limps off.

Ravian and Kars are sitting on the edge of the deck again, with their feet poking through the railing. Kars has Sol under his jumper. He shivers now and then because her shell feels so cold against his stomach.

Ravian gazes at the horizon. Can he see wings moving in the distance? Is Marvin on his way back to the *Night Raider*? He's been away for four days now – is that a good sign or a bad sign? Ravian sighs. The boys look at the sea, waiting for a good moment to release Sol into the water. The waves aren't high now. The day has actually turned out calm. The water is still swarming with jellyfish, though. Wherever they look, there are those nasty blue blobs.

'Kind of yucky, huh?'

'Mm-hm.' Kars makes a face.

'Should we let her into the water here?' asks Ravian. Kars doesn't reply, just looks doubtfully at the blubbery sea under his feet.

'Kars?'

'Yeah. I was just thinking about how horrible it would be to swim in that stuff, but I don't suppose a turtle would mind . . .'

Ravian chuckles.

'No, for a turtle it'd be like swimming in ice cream or in a big bag of chips!'

Kars laughs at that idea. Ravian can hear his friend's stomach rumbling.

'Go on, then.' He looks around to check that Bank hasn't suddenly appeared. Then he takes Sol out from under his jumper. He holds her up and the boys both look at her for a moment.

'Bye, sweet Sol.' Ravian strokes her head.

'Bye, my friend,' says Kars. 'Come back and visit, won't you?'

The turtle's beady eyes blink happily. Kars puts her back in the oyster net and lowers it into the water. As she swims away, she looks back at the boys and then vanishes into her pool of ice cream.

They watch her go.

'What was up with Bank? Why was he acting so strangely?' asks Ravian with a chuckle.

But Kars doesn't laugh.

'When he's like that, there's usually something going on,' he says in a worried voice. Then, after a brief silence, he adds, 'Maybe we shouldn't have let Sol go yet. I've been sailing with him for a year, but sometimes things happen that I've never seen before.

When Bank's like that, then . . . yes . . . I don't know. He hasn't seen everything himself, of course. But he knows all the stories.'

'But how? He doesn't ever speak to anyone but us, does he?' Ravian asks.

'Not any more, no.'

Ravian looks back at the mass of jellyfish. He can't understand why Bank is so bothered about them. He knows that sometimes as many as a hundred jellyfish wash up on the beach in Rottenherring. Bank hasn't been on a beach for quite a few years, so maybe he's forgotten what it's like. Ravian studies the swarming blobs from his safe spot behind the railing. It's so strange that jellyfish can't move by themselves but are moved by the sea.

'Hmm. So, the jellyfish's muscle is actually the power of the sea,' Ravian says. But Kars has stood up and he doesn't reply.

'I'm just going to fetch Bank,' he says hesitantly.

12

THE JELLYFISH

The *Night Raider* suddenly starts rocking dramatically. Even Bank, who's come back on deck, can't stand upright, although he's still the one with the best sea legs.

'What's going on?' Ravian shouts at Kars. 'Is the sea angry again? Is this what Bank kept talking about?'

Kars wipes his hand over his face and doesn't reply. He walks towards the mast. The sky is bright blue, and the sun is shining happily. There's no way a storm can be coming.

'Um, is this another curse?' asks Ravian. He tries to sound as casual as possible.

He looks over the rail at the sea. But the waves are pretty calm too. There's no angry swirling and whirling this time.

'It's as if –' Ravian feels his stomach churning – 'something is throwing us back and forth!'

'Yes . . .' the pirate begins. Then he suddenly falls over, up by the bow of the ship, where the ship is at its lowest. Is that because the pirate's so heavy? No, of course not.

Slowly, with a squelching sound, a purplish-white creature appears over the rail.

Ravian's legs feel like they're about to collapse like jelly.

The creature grabs hold of the edge of the rail – just above Bank's head, who doesn't seem to have noticed yet.

'W-what is that?' stammers Ravian. Another squelchy creature has just appeared beside him, and it's climbing up over the rail. And there's another one! They're really long and about as thick as Ravian's arm, with frilly stuff draped around them like skirts, and

181

they seem to be made of some sort of squishy, spongy substance.

They wrap themselves firmly around the rail, and the ship starts to rock even harder. Ravian quickly runs to the mast, where Kars is standing. The violent shaking makes it really hard to move in a straight line. Every time the ship swings one way or the other, Ravian's stomach lurches along with it. Kars reaches his hand out to Ravian and grabs him just before he falls. Ravian can hold on to the mast now, and those scary creatures – what kind of animals are they? – can't reach him here.

'What are they?' Ravian shouts. 'Animals? Monsters? Do you think it was the sea who sent them?'

A grey cloud moves slowly over the *Night Raider*. Kars holds on tightly to the mast. Slowly shaking his head, he takes a closer look at the creatures.

'They look like tentacles,' he says with a frown. 'Like the jellyfish's tentacles.'

'But that big?' squeaks Ravian. 'That's impossible, isn't it?'

'Aaargh!' yells Bank. 'Blast it!'

The tentacle that just came up onto the deck by the pirate has hit him on the forehead. A huge reddish-purple blister is spreading over half of his face.

'Portugal!' Bank screams, clutching his head.

Ravian looks in surprise at Kars.

'Portugal?' he shouts.

Kars shakes his head. He has no idea either.

'The monster jellyfish of Portugal!' shouts the pirate. 'He's here!'

Wailing and yelling, Bank collapses onto the deck again.

'He's found me!'

'Come on,' Kars says to Ravian. 'We have to do something!'

With careful steps, Kars walks over to Bank. He can barely keep his balance.

'You have to move away from it, Bank! Come on!' shouts Kars.

But the pirate isn't listening. He's crippled with pain and clutching his blistered face.

Kars calls Ravian over. But Ravian doesn't want to abandon the mast. He's safe here, and this is where he feels the rocking least. Going over to the screaming pirate, with those poisonous tentacles slithering around him, doesn't seem like a very sensible plan.

'What should we do?' Kars shouts at Ravian when he doesn't move.

'About the sting?' Ravian shouts back. For a moment he imagines having to apply his 'miracle medicine' to Bank's face. That certainly wouldn't be a good idea.

'No, about that monster!' Kars points in panic at the tentacle that's slowly creeping across the deck.

Ravian thinks, but he can't come up with anything. With every wobble and every sway, he feels more sick. He can only think about home. Going home, going home. On dry land. Oh, if only he'd stayed at home. If only he was on his dune now, or on his own beach, with his feet safely on the sand, together with

Marvin . . . If only he was washing glasses for Nell at that stupid pub. If only Lasse hadn't been a fisherman . . . If only it had never been his birthday. If only he'd never heard the story of Bank and this cursed ship. It would have been sad if he'd never met Kars, though. Ravian shuts his eyes for a moment and imagines that he's on land and that nothing's moving. That helps a bit, but then he just feels even more sick with his eyes shut.

'There's no time to lose, Rav!' shouts Kars.

The tentacles are crawling all across the deck now. There are thick trails of slime dripping from the rail and everything else they've touched. Their grip seems to be getting even stronger, and the big jellyfish is tossing the ship further and further, from side to side. Ravian's head is thumping away. What should they do? What can you do to fight a beast like that?

Kars runs to Bank and leans over the pirate, who's still bellowing at the top of his lungs. The knife he always carries is sticking out of his belt. Without saying anything, Kars grabs the knife, and like a knight drawing his sword, he pulls it from its leather sheath and holds it in the air. The pirate doesn't say anything. He doesn't even notice because of the pain. He's silent now, and looks as if he might pass out at any moment.

With one quick movement, Kars thrusts the knife into the tentacle that's squirming across the deck. After the stab, the tentacle stops and twitches a bit, but as soon as Kars pulls the knife out it starts advancing again.

'It's not working!' yells Ravian. 'And you're getting your hand far too close to it. You need to be careful, Kars! Or you'll get a massive blister, too!'

'But what else can we do?' screams Kars, stabbing the tentacle again with full force.

'Stop! Stop!' Ravian shouts frantically. He takes a deep breath, counts to three, braces himself and then lets go of the mast. Concentrating very hard, he makes his way to Kars. He has to take small steps so that he can move with the swaying ship.

'I don't feel sick. I'm not scared,' he whispers. Whenever it looks as if he's about to fall over, he grabs hold of something to steady him. It's going pretty well, as he stumbles and crawls along, keeping a close eye on where the tentacles are. 'I can't fall into the water. I can't fall into the water. I can't leave the ship. I can't leave the ship. Nothing bad's going to happen to me. Nothing bad's going to happen to me.'

Kars pulls the knife out of the tentacle and raises it, ready to stab again.

'No, Kars!' shouts Ravian. He grabs Kars's arm with both hands to stop him. 'Can't you see it's not doing any good?'

Kars's forehead is sweaty. His blond hair is plastered to his brow. He looks desperately at Ravian, as if the sea has just washed away the last of his hope.

Slowly, he lowers his arm and drops the knife. Together they look helplessly at the chunk of monster and the pirate lying beside it. The ship is normally held in the clutches of the sea, but it's now in the clutches of the jellyfish.

The jellyfish . . . Tentacles . . . Jellyfish sting! Yes!

'I've got it!' shouts Ravian, looking around the deck.

'What?' asks Kars.

'Come on!' Ravian drags Kars with him. 'We have to go to the hold. I need you to help me carry it!'

Kars still doesn't understand what's going on, but he runs after Ravian, who has plucked up all his courage and is running downstairs into the hold, as he is hurled this way and that.

'Where is it?' Ravian mutters to himself.

'Hello?! Hey, Rav! What are you looking for?' says Kars.

'Remember the tentacle that was stuck to Bank's leg?' says Ravian, running around frantically.

'Yes.'

Ravian stops at a big wooden crate and pulls off the lid. His eyes light up. Ta-da!

'Rum!' says Kars. 'Of course!'

They grab as many bottles as they can carry. Kars goes first and, staggering, he reaches the stairs. He's much faster than Ravian. Keeping your balance is even more difficult when your arms are full. One of the bottles is about to fall. Ravian can't hold it. **SMASH!** It shatters on the floor. Ravian feels like screaming, but he takes a deep breath. Then he looks through one of the portholes, where a fat, squishy tentacle is clamped to the glass. It releases its hold and moves on.

The water is still full of the little jellyfish, like an army protecting their monstrous father. Ravian narrows his eyes. Is he seeing that right? Are the jellyfish giving off light? A huge wave crashes against the side of the ship. The water sounds so different with all those blobs in it. Ravian has paused to watch for far too long. He has to keep going. But then he hears the sea whispering again:

. . . haul it in, guard it well . . .
. . . and wait till you've won . . .

Ravian frowns. Is the jellyfish part of the riddle? Is the monstrous creature hauling the ship in? Where's he going to guard them? At the bottom of the sea?

The sloshing jellyfish outside the window are making Ravian's stomach slosh about too.

'Hey, come on,' he says out loud to himself. Keep going, before that giant jellyfish pulls the *Night Raider* down with it.

On the deck, Ravian opens the first bottle and empties it onto the tentacle that has wound its way furthest onto the deck. The tentacle shrivels, twists and twitches. It shakes and trembles – and then it retreats. Just as the tentacle is about to fall off the ship, it grabs onto one of the bars of the railing at the last moment. Quickly, Ravian pulls the cork from another bottle and pours it out onto the tentacle. Once again, all the muscles twitch – and then it's finally gone. It lets go and falls back into the sea.

Kars is trying to get rid of another of the slimy tentacles that's crept onto the deck. It takes one whole bottle and most of another. And then that tentacle falls, defeated, back into the sea. Kars cheers, but the relief doesn't last long.

When the boys look around, they see that they're nowhere near done. All over the railing, more enormous tentacles are climbing on board.

Pirate Bank is still groaning away in his corner. He's a pirate with a scary reputation, but when it comes down to it, he's not really that tough at all. And he hasn't even realised yet that his precious supply of rum is being wasted.

With his hands in his hair, Kars looks at Ravian, who is pouring rum onto all the tentacles he finds.

'Come on, Kars!' Ravian keeps pouring so that Kars doesn't lose motivation. This seems to be an endless task too, but they have to keep going, or they'll soon be sinking into the depths with that jellyfish. Ravian is terrified of the tentacles that he's drowning in alcohol, but drowning in the sea himself would be far worse. But . . . can the ship actually sink? What about the curse? Ravian shakes his head. He can't take any risks. There's only one way to find out if the ship can sink and Ravian can't afford to wait for that. By then, it'll be too late.

13

CRATES OF RUM

Kars runs back to the hold to fetch more bottles. He gives some to Ravian. But every time they pour rum onto one of the tentacles and it disappears, another one appears somewhere else on the deck. As if the jellyfish has an infinite number of them.

'This is never going to end!' shouts Ravian. It feels like he's pouring rum over his newfound confidence too. He's starting to lose hope.

'Emptying all these bottles will take too long,' Kars shouts back. 'We need to smash them onto the tentacles. That'll be quicker!'

Ravian nods. With a big swing of his arm, he throws the bottle in his hand as hard as he can onto a squirming tentacle. It works! It hits much harder too, so the thing retreats faster.

'Look! It's scared!' Ravian shouts proudly. Kars joins in.

SMASH! SMASH! SMASH!

As fast as they can, the boys throw all the bottles, breaking them on the tentacles, and taking turns to dash downstairs to fetch more bottles so they can keep going. The tentacles dart away like shy little bunny rabbits.

FLOP! FLAP! FLOP!

The rocking of the ship is slowing, too. The tentacle in the corner near Pirate Bank is still wriggling away, though. Kars takes two bottles under his arm and smashes one of them right in front of Bank.

'What on earth are you doing, you idiot?' the pirate howls. He seems to have come back to his senses. Struggling to his feet, he snatches the other bottle from Kars's hand.

'But look!' Kars points at the writhing tentacle. The pirate stares in surprise and opens the bottle.

And he takes a big swig.

Unbelievable!

Then Kars wrestles back the bottle and, before Bank can protest, breaks that one too.

Bank gives him a furious shove, but then they hear the splash of the tentacle falling into the sea. Bank and Kars pause and look at each other for a couple of seconds. Then, at the same time, they go and lean over the rail to watch the tentacle disappearing into the waves.

'Oh no,' says Kars with a deep, despairing sigh. 'Rav,' he calls, 'Rav, we're still not there!'

Ravian comes running and leans over the rail with them. There might not be any tentacles left on board the ship, but the sides are covered with them! They're wrapped firmly around the boat. Ravian's jaw drops, and his heart sinks. They were so close.

Biting his lip, he tries not to cry.

The army of small jellyfish is still moving around the ship in the wildly waving sea. They seem to have little lights inside their bodies. Any minute, they'll go on the attack too or come flying onto the ship. Nothing would surprise Ravian now. But he can worry about that later. Don't give up. Keep going. He has to. For Marvin, for Lasse, even for Bank.

For Kars.

For himself.

He holds up his last bottle, ready to attack.

'It's not enough,' he says quietly to himself.

'We need the whole crate!' Kars shouts at him, and he beckons Ravian to go and fetch it with him from the hold.

'No! You sneaky little rats! Don't use up all my rum! Not my bottles!' the pirate yells angrily.

The boys don't listen to him. Once they're all safe, maybe he'll see they were right. At least that's what Ravian's hoping. There's still a full crate of rum down there with the supplies in the hold.

'But we can't carry that crate up there, not with just the two of us,' squeaks Ravian.

'Yes, we can,' says Kars. 'Come on, we're strong.' He grabs one of the handles. 'Will you hold the other one? I'll lead.'

Ravian tries to lift it and gets the crate a tiny bit off the ground. They give each other a worried look.

'In small bursts,' Kars says encouragingly. 'Come on!'

They walk a few steps with the crate before putting it down again. And another few steps, and a rest. They bump into the walls and trip and drop the crate. But they bravely keep going.

When they reach the stairs, it gets even trickier.

'I'll go first. You push, and I'll pull,' says Kars.

With difficulty, they get the crate up the stairs, one step at a time. And finally the two boys are standing up on deck with the huge crate of rum, puffing and panting.

'Okay,' says Kars, 'come on. Grab a bottle in each hand. I'll go to the port side; you go to starboard. Then we'll lean over the rail and throw the bottles so they smash against the side of the ship. That way we'll get the most tentacles in one go.'

Ravian runs over to his post on the starboard side and throws the bottle down onto the ship with all his might. It shatters and the rum sprays over the tentacles, which twitch and shrivel – and in some places they start letting go.

'Quickly!' says Kars. The boys run from the crate to the rail and back.

The pirate can't bear to watch his rum being looted. 'Stop it, you couple of meddling manatees!' he yells at them. 'Argh, eel entrails!' But Kars and Ravian pretend not to hear him and bravely battle on.

SMASH! SMASH! FLOP!

The rum-covered tentacles finally let go of the ship. The liquid soaks into the wood and drips down the sides of the ship, so the tentacles won't want to come back now. Slowly, the rocking of the ship seems to lessen, and when Ravian peers over the rail again he sees that all the tentacles are indeed gone.

At last!

The boys stand still, waiting to see if they need to keep up the bottle bombardment.

'Please!' Bank yells at them. He has staggered over to the crate. He sits beside it, holding his arms over it to protect his rum. 'Enough! That's enough!'

Kars stands with his bottle ready to throw and looks all around the ship to make sure there are no tentacles stuck anywhere. It is still as if the ship is being held somehow. They can't feel the natural swell of the sea.

Ravian goes to stand beside him. He has the worst sea legs, of course, but that makes him all the more sensitive to any strange movements.

'There!' Kars shouts, pointing at the bow of the ship. One tentacle is still holding on tightly. This one is the biggest of all. There seem to be sparks shooting off it, and the sides are glowing with purplish-white light. The two boys run over to it. It's in a difficult spot to hit. Kars throws first, but just misses. Then Ravian throws. Another near miss. The tentacle is in trouble – it's twitching and quivering, but it's not letting go. Kars throws another bottle, just above the tentacle. All the rum slowly drips down the wood and onto the monstrous tentacle.

'Maybe we should both throw at the same time!' suggests Ravian. They hold their bottles ready, and Ravian starts counting down. 'Three . . . two . . . one!' and

SMASH SMASH!

The two bottles land with enormous force on the last tentacle. It convulses and shakes violently. Then it turns pale and, beaten, it falls into the water, purple sparks flying off it.

The *Night Raider* is free. Ravian looks at the sea with wide eyes. It's actually a beautiful sight. In the water beneath the ship, he and Kars can finally see the body of the giant jellyfish, which is shot through with golden threads. It's giving off light too! Even now that it's defeated and sinking limply to the bottom.

'Let's get out of here!' yells Kars. He runs to Bank, who's still draped over his crate of rum. Kars grabs him by the shoulders and gives him a good shake.

'We have to get away, Bank, and fast! Before that jellyfish recovers and grabs hold of us again!'

The pirate finally seems to understand. He scrambles to his feet and, groaning away, he takes hold of the ropes on the mast.

Ravian looks at the sea again. The defeated tentacles are still floating in the waves here and there.

But slowly, one by one, they drown like dead snakes in the deep sea.

The lights of the jellyfish army seem to be fading too. Their father is defeated, so why would they shine their lights now? They disappear, following the thick tentacles into the depths.

Pirate Bank turns the sails, so that the wind blows full into them from the side and the ship can sail at its fastest. The clouds slowly retreat. The sea is calm again and has returned to her normal dark-blue colour. No sparks, no lights, no monsters. Kars is standing at the wheel and, full speed ahead, they sail away. Away from the army of jellyfish, away from the monster's arms and to a stretch of open sea.

Ravian is relieved but still full of questions. Was that really what the riddle was about? And what did those lines mean, the ones about the leaf in the wind and the top bright with sun? Have they beaten the sea now because the jellyfish couldn't hold on to them? Is beating the sea something that anyone should want to do?

He sighs and sits down next to Bank. Now that he can take a good look at him, he sees that his face is badly damaged. It's just one big blister. But he seems to have forgotten his anger. He even gives Ravian a friendly nod.

'Hey, you,' he says. 'That was pretty clever.'

Ravian smiles.

'But if you ever touch my rum again, I'll have to keelhaul you.'

Ravian's smile disappears.

'Keelhaul?'

Kars shakes his head. Then the pirate bursts out laughing. Really loud. So loud that the ship starts rocking again.

14

INTET AT TABE

'Look, that's better!' Bank shouts happily. Kars tips the fishing net upside down and a big haul of fish lands on the deck. For a whole day, they've been sailing fast, without looking back and without talking; all three of them staring ahead, still shocked and exhausted.

'We'll have a slap-up dinner tonight. We've earned it, haven't we, men?' Bank is cheery. He's still limping a bit and the blister on his face is horrible. The edges are already healing, but it's red and swollen and there's pus coming out. It must be really sore. But fishing seems to be doing him some good.

'Will you start frying them?' the pirate asks Kars. Kars nods.

When the crew have filled their hungry tummies, the three of them sit together on deck. The pirate has made a fire in a brazier. He's sitting on a box and holding his hands to the flames to warm them. It's dark now, and bright stars are shining in the sky. Kars is lying on his back, looking up at them. Ravian is lying beside him on his stomach, staring at the fire.

Where's Marvin got to? He's been away for five days now. Nothing's happened to him, has it? Ravian tries to imagine that Marvin's found Lasse's boat and that the two of them are now sailing together to the *Night Raider*. And that they're singing all of Lasse's songs while they hoist the sails, brave the waves and, using Marvin's excellent sense of direction, sail swiftly back to Ravian. And that's what's taking so long.

'How are your wounds doing?' Kars asks Bank.

'That miracle medicine really helped,' he says. 'What was in it?'

Ravian glances at Kars, who can barely hold in his laughter.

'Oh, it's a family secret. An old recipe. Nothing special. Herbs, water, you know, um . . .'

'Well, thank you anyway,' Bank says, interrupting him. 'Or should I say, "Bank you"?'

Ravian smiles at Kars. It's a wonderful evening. The sea is calm and there's a gentle breeze.

'Hey, lad, what was your name again?'

Pirates clearly don't have the best of memories.

'Ravian.'

Bank nods.

'Ravian . . . And where do you come from?'

'From a small village by a harbour. It's called Rottenherring.'

Bank's jaw drops and the bottle he's drinking from falls from his hands. With a dull thud, it lands on the planks, luckily unbroken.

'Rottenherring?'

Ravian frowns. 'Yes. Do you know it, captain?'

Bank stares at him for a few seconds before shaking his head.

'No,' he says, a bit too quickly, the way people do when they're lying. 'Never heard of it. But I meant how did you end up on my ship? And call me Bank.'

'I, um . . .' Ravian begins. He sighs quietly. He doesn't want to have to think again about how long his dad's been away. Kars gives him an encouraging pat on the shoulder.

'I'm looking for my father,' he says.

'Your father? Have you lost him?' asks Bank.

'He's gone away,' says Ravian. 'He went to sea, and he still hasn't come back. He's a fisherman, so he's actually always at sea, but he comes home every year for my birthday. Not this time, though. And, um . . . someone told me about your ship and said maybe he was trapped here. So I came to look for him. And I'm such an idiot that I got stuck here myself.'

'Ah, such irony,' says Bank, staring at the deck.

Ravian nods. He doesn't know what the word means, but it sounds nice. As if Bank understands him. For a while, they sit in silence. The fire in the brazier crackles gently. Ravian finds the sound of the waves breaking against the ship kind of calming now, as long as he doesn't think about it for too long.

'What about you?' Ravian asks Bank, surprised at his own daring.

Bank looks at him. 'How did I end up on this ship?'

'Yes, I mean . . . Where are you actually from?'

Bank doesn't reply. Has Ravian gone too far?

'I was once looking for my dad too,' Bank suddenly begins. 'My father was a big, muscular man, maybe even a bit scary. But he was really nice to me. Like your dad, he spent a lot of time away at sea. But my father wasn't a fisherman. He was a pirate. He stole ships and plundered cities. He looted treasure and jewels and pearls. When I was ten, I slipped out of bed one night and hid on his ship. He was furious when he found me. By that time, we were already on the high seas. So he had to take me with him. My mother would never let me go, you see. And neither would my father, in fact. Far too dangerous. My parents weren't together any more. "He's not to be trusted," my mother always said, but I was allowed to see him when he happened to be around.

'I thought it was terrifying on board with all those sailors, but they turned out to be pretty nice – well, to me at least, because of who my father was. I had the time of my life. I finally got to know my dad and saw for myself who he was instead of hearing stories about him. I was on the ship for six months before I was sent home. They were going on a long journey that was too dangerous for me as a boy. Even though I'd proved myself. My father said that it made him weaker, me being there. He wanted to protect me. If I was there, he had something to lose. Pirates need to have nothing to lose. He'd actually had that tattooed on his chest in big letters in Danish: INTET AT TABE.'

Bank stares into the flames, as if he can see it all playing out in front of his eyes.

'So that was that,' he continues. 'I went back home, back to my mother and back to my normal life. But I hated it. I missed the sea, and my dad, and his crew. For years, I got up at dawn and stood on the lookout to see if he was returning, but his ship never appeared on that blasted horizon.'

'That sounds familiar,' says Ravian.

Bank smiles.

'Ah, lad, the fate of a sailor's child . . .' And then he falls silent. Ravian understands what he means.

'And when I grew up, I was free to join another ship. It was in the harbour and the captain was a few men short. So I seized the chance. I thought I'd be sure to meet my father somewhere one day. Stupid idea, of course. After years and years had gone by, I realised that I . . . wasn't mixing with the right people, as it were. An ordinary sailor never meets a pirate he can sit and have a drink or two with. And so I decided to become a pirate instead. Anyway, it's a long story. I spent some time on land for a while too, after I'd given up the search for my father. But the sea, oh, the sea . . . I couldn't stay away from her for long. So, I, um . . . acquired this ship, shall we say.'

The boys smile.

'Ah yes, acquired! Nicely put!' says Kars.

'Ssh,' says Bank, chuckling, 'I'd rather not remind the sea about that. What I really wanted was to be alone, to have a whole ship to myself, as soon as I realised my dad would never return. I felt betrayed by everyone and everything. Since then, all I've wanted is to be happy in a place where I'm completely alone – the sea and me, and no one else. I think it made my dad feel closer somehow. But it seems the sea didn't agree with my plan to be alone.'

For a moment, they silently watch the flames and the glowing logs. Pretty strange that such a big pirate could be controlled like that by the power of the sea.

'Bank?' asks Ravian. 'What are those riddles all about?'

Bank looks at him with a vexed expression.

'How do you know about the riddles? What have you heard?' he says.

'There was a voice inside a shell after we ate the oysters. I held it to my ear and the voice said: *Leaf in the wind, top bright with sun, haul it in, guard it well, and wait till you've won.* And it happened again yesterday when I was in the hold, looking at the jellyfish in the sea.'

'So you're in on it already, are you? And? Did you understand what it meant?' the pirate asks eagerly.

'Um, no,' replies Ravian. 'You?'

'No. I don't even know who the riddle's meant for. For us? For someone else? Why won't anyone solve it? And then she can move on to the next mystery. Stupid sea! And it's so vague. *Leaf in the wind, top bright with sun.* That's always true, isn't it? I think so. Or at least usually. Leaves blow on the wind, and the sun generally shines on the top of things. Right?'

Ravian nods.

'*Haul it in, guard it well, and wait till you've won*. Haul in what? Won what?' Bank sighs and throws up his hands.

'I thought it might have something to do with that jellyfish. That it was going to haul us in and guard us well,' says Ravian. 'But when we got free, I wasn't so sure.'

Kars glances at Ravian.

'I don't think the sea has riddles for her creatures,' Kars says decisively, 'only for people.'

Bank nods thoughtfully.

'I've sometimes thought it was just to drive us sailors even crazier,' he says then. 'You know, to have fun plaguing us. I wouldn't put that past the sea. To come up with a riddle without an answer.'

Kars sighs.

'Didn't I tell you?' he says quietly to Ravian.

'What?' growls the pirate.

'He said I should talk to you about it,' says Ravian quickly.

'Well, that's a foolish idea, isn't it? I don't have a clue!'

Ravian really wants to find out more about the riddle. And about the curse. And about the *Night Raider*. Does Bank know more about it? He hesitates for a moment but then decides to ask anyway.

'Bank, can the *Night Raider* actually sink?'

Bank looks at Ravian as if he's just said that he thinks rum's disgusting.

'Why? Did you have plans?' he asks.

'No, no,' Ravian replies, furiously shaking his head. 'I was just wondering. If we could have sunk and drowned yesterday. You know, if we hadn't managed to beat the jellyfish.'

Bank turns down the corners of his mouth and stares at the moonlit sea.

'I don't know,' he says quietly. 'It's not as if the sea bothers to explain all her rules.'

Ravian nods.

When the fire has almost gone out, Bank stands up.

'Right, men, I'm going to sleep for a few hours. It'll be good for my blisters. That idiotic riddle is making them itch even more. Did you have to start talking about it?' he says irritably as he heads inside.

'Sweet dreams,' says Ravian with a smile. The pirate grunts. It seems he's no longer in the mood for sharing.

'Wow,' says Ravian when Bank has left. 'That was quite a story!'

Kars nods.

'Did you know all of that already?'

'Yes, I've had nights like this with him before. When he opens up and talks about all kinds of adventures he's had at sea. He's told me about his sweetheart, for instance, and about this one time when his father taught him to swordfight and they had to take on a sea serpent. I told you he'd warm up after a while, didn't I?'

'Yes, you did,' replies Ravian. 'Is that why you tried to stop me when I wanted to come onto the *Night Raider*? Because you were scared it would make Bank angry again?'

'No, of course not! I thought it was horrible for you and that you'd get stuck here and could never set foot on land.'

'But you didn't even know me. So why did you care?' asks Ravian.

'Well, no . . . but you seemed . . . nice.'

Ravian is silent. He turns onto his back so that they can look at the stars together. Kars's shoulder feels warm against his own.

It's actually not too bad here on board.

'What would you do first if you could go back on land?' Ravian asks after a while.

'Ooh, no idea,' replies Kars. 'Eat an ice cream. With whipped cream on top!'

Ravian laughs.

'No, I'd buy a big axe and try to open that secret door downstairs. Or a skeleton key. You know, one of those keys that fits any lock. Or I could just ask a locksmith.'

Ravian chuckles.

'What about you?' Kars turns onto his side and looks at Ravian. 'If the curse is ever lifted, what are you going to do?'

Ravian thinks about it.

'I'd look for Dad and Marvin and go back home. And pick up my old life there. Playing games, making music, lighting campfires and looking at the stars long into the night. I'd make my dad spend more time at home. Maybe I'd take on an extra job so that he wouldn't have to go to sea so often.' Ravian grins at the thought.

Kars is quiet. Very quiet. He lies on his back again. Ravian peeps at him out of the corner of his eye.

'What about me?' Kars finally stammers. His voice sounds fragile, as if there's a lump in his throat.

'You?' replies Ravian. 'I can help you to find your old home, if you like.'

Kars shoots to his feet like a cannonball.

'Hey, where are you going? What's wrong? I can't decide for you what you're going to do, can I?' says Ravian. Kars heads inside.

Did Ravian say something wrong?

In the cabin, Kars is lying in the dark with his face to the wall and his blanket pulled almost completely over his head. Ravian picks up a lantern and walks into the room.

'Hey, Kars. Are you asleep?'

Kars doesn't reply.

Ravian hesitates. Should he go away?

But he decides instead to sit down on the edge of Kars's bed.

Ravian takes a deep breath.

'What's wrong?'

'Nothing,' Kars says grumpily.

'Okay, but you sound pretty angry.'

'So?'

'Was it me who upset you?' asks Ravian. He doesn't receive a reply.

He gently rests his hand on Kars's arm.

'Go away,' Kars says quietly.

'But I . . .' Ravian begins. 'What did I do wrong? Hey, come out of that hole for a moment and talk to me.'

Kars still doesn't say anything, but then he turns around.

'Hi,' says Ravian.

'Hi,' sighs Kars.

'What's up?'

'I just thought that . . . No, forget about it, this'll probably sound really stupid.' Kars goes to pull the blankets over his head again, but Ravian stops him.

'No, wait, don't go back in there!' he calls. 'I never think you're stupid. In fact, I always think that you're . . . so clever that it makes me feel really stupid in comparison,' he adds.

'Well, yeah, that is kind of stupid of you,' says Kars. Both of them smile.

'What were you going to say?' Ravian asks.

'I was just hoping that I . . . that I could . . . Oh, I don't know. That, if we ever get off this ship, we'll go off and do something together.' Kars looks at the ceiling of the cabin.

'But, Kars, that's what I really want too! I didn't mean it to come out like that. Just because I want to be with Dad and Marvin, that doesn't mean that I . . .'

Ravian's legs feel weak. Like jelly. A bit like those strange tentacles that slithered across the deck.

He takes a deep breath. '. . . that I don't want to be with you, does it?'

'Doesn't it?'

'Oh, I'm an idiot . . .' says Ravian. 'Sorry. Maybe I just said it because I miss them so much.'

He'd miss Kars at least as much if he were gone. But of course he doesn't dare to say that.

'Really?'

'Of course!' says Ravian. He smiles. 'Sorry, Kars, I didn't mean to upset you.'

'No,' says Kars, 'I know. It's okay.'

* * *

The next morning, the boys are standing at the front of the ship, looking out over the water. They don't say anything, just smile at each other now and then. They've been there for a while. The sea is calm, the sun is shining brightly and there are beautiful, unthreatening clouds shaped like dolphins, as if they're just swimming past in the sky.

The sea, the sky, the land. Ravian didn't know they had such dark and magical stories to tell.

He stares at the water. Although it still looks scary and murky and far too deep, he does feel a little calmer inside. He doesn't immediately get lost in gloomy thoughts about everything that could go wrong if he fell into it. Even the gentle swaying of the ship feels a bit like the rocking of a cradle now – it's really quite soothing.

Out of nowhere, a seagull lands on the rail.

'Marvin!' Kars exclaims.

Ravian raises his gaze and finds himself looking at the happy face of his oldest friend.

'**KROEEEEEEE KROOTKROOT KRIEE,**' shrieks Marvin. It's their special call.

'Marvin! You were away for so long! Where have you been and . . .'

Ravian looks at Marvin in amazement.

'What's that in your beak? Is that . . .'

He can't believe it.

'Is that Dad's ring?'

15

THE STORM

Ravian runs across the deck, waving his arms in the air.

'WOO-HOO!' he shouts. 'Marvin! This is amazing!'

Marvin, who seems to have forgotten how tired he is after his long flight, does happy flips in the air. He's so proud.

'Kars! Do you see this?' Ravian has Lasse's gold ring firmly between his fingers and holds it up to show Kars.

'Look, his name is engraved on the inside!'

Kars laughs out loud.

'Yes! I can see that, you idiot!' he says, but Ravian has already darted off.

'Marvin, oh, lovely Marvin! How's Dad doing? Where did you find him? Was he okay?' Ravian says, chattering away.

Marvin tilts his head.

'Can you take us to him? Do you remember how to get there? It must have been a really long way, eh? Or it wouldn't have taken you six days. Or did you spend a long time with Dad?'

Marvin flies up and points with his wing in the direction he came from.

'You'll take us there?' Ravian asks cheerfully.

Marvin nods again, enthusiastically flapping his wings together, as if he's clapping.

'Take us where?' shouts Bank, who comes running from the other side of the ship. He's been watching the boys and the seagull. 'What's all this about? What's going on?'

Ravian runs over to him.

'Bank, look!' he says, beaming as he shows him the ring. The pirate's eyes light up too, as they do when a pirate sees shiny gold things.

'Ah! The bird's found some treasure! Why didn't you say so?' says Bank. He grins from ear to ear and looks up at Marvin. 'Where are we heading, sailor?'

'No, no, no!' Ravian says, interrupting him. 'That ring belongs to my dad! Marvin's found my dad!'

Pirate Bank raises his eyebrows. 'I take it Marvin's the bird?'

Ravian nods frantically. 'Yes, and now he can take us to my dad. Or at least show us the way. If we sail after him, then –'

'We can't just go sailing somewhere else!' the pirate shouts grumpily.

Ravian frowns. 'Why not?'

'Because I say so.'

'But why not?'

'Because I don't know how far it will be. And there was a new moon last night, which is why we could see the stars so well. That means we're halfway through the month and that we have to go back to Deaf Diederik's harbour soon. Especially after the two of you used up nearly all my rum supplies!'

Ravian rolls his eyes. 'Yes, but that was to save all of us, wasn't it?'

'I don't care. I need my rum. I can't risk being without it for a whole month!' Bank snorts.

Ravian looks at him for a long time. He can't believe it. His fingertips are tingling with rage, and he clenches his fist around the ring. How can Bank be so mean? So unsympathetic? Just when Ravian thought they were getting along and getting to know each other a bit, he's gone back to being a heartless old pirate. Ravian struggles to find the right words. What he really wants to do is yell at Bank, but he doesn't know what to say. With an angry grunt, he turns around and walks back to Kars.

'I'll talk to him,' says Kars, patting Ravian on the shoulder. He takes a few steps towards the pirate and says in his friendliest voice, 'Hey, Bank, what's the matter?'

Bank just growls.

Kars takes him firmly by the shoulders, forcing the pirate to look at him.

'Didn't you lose your father too? You never found him. You still haven't! And Ravian . . . You like him, don't you? You think he's a good lad? You said so yesterday.'

The pirate shrugs. He clearly doesn't know what to say.

'Well, now *he* has the chance to see his father again! That's the best news you can imagine. You of all people should understand that.'

Bank gives a little nod.

'Come on, Bank.' Kars talks to the angry pirate like an old friend.

Ravian's boiling anger subsides when he sees the calm look on Kars's face.

'Okay, then,' Bank mutters. 'But what about my rum?'

'We'll come up with something. I promise. Anyway, I have no idea where we'll end up. Maybe they'll have the best rum you've ever tasted!'

That cheers the pirate up a bit. A little smile appears on his lips. Then he gives a deep sigh, pushes up his sleeves and nods at Ravian and Marvin.

'Right, then, seagull. Show us the way!'

When they've been sailing for a few hours – Marvin up ahead, Bank at the wheel, Kars by the sails and Ravian fearless in the bow at the front of the ship – a big shadow falls over the *Night Raider*.

'Is it getting dark already? We haven't been sailing for that long, have we?' Ravian mutters to himself. It shouldn't be anywhere near evening yet. He looks at the sky. A big dark-grey cloud has moved over the sun. Ravian looks over his shoulder at Kars. His eyes are on the sky too. They look at each other with serious faces.

'Storm on the way!' shouts Kars. Almost immediately, there's a huge gust of wind. Ravian's black curls fly up with a whoosh. The sails rattle in the wind. The ropes slap against the mast and the side of the ship.

'Look out, men!' Bank shouts from the helm. 'The wind is the sea's humble henchman. He does whatever she tells him!'

Ravian watches the wild waves, which grow bigger every time the wind caresses them. Huge raindrops fall like a furious legion out of the dark sky into the sea and onto the ship. Ravian makes a firm fist around Lasse's ring, which he's hung on a piece of string around his neck.

Marvin squints to protect his eyes from the sharp sea wind. Gathering his courage, he flies on with strong beats of his wings. Onwards! He can't give up now!

For a while, everyone on the ship waits in silence, while the sea and the wind make their loud voices heard. Ravian, Kars and Bank stand strong at their posts. Bank has his legs far apart so that he can keep his balance at the helm. Kars holds on to the rigging, and Ravian clasps the rail.

The *Night Raider* and her crew can take a beating. They know that. They've already had to prove it.

But the storm is getting worse. The sea wants more of a fight. Big waves swirl and whirl in the dark depths, spinning the *Night Raider* to the left and the right.

Ravian keeps his eyes closed and whispers to himself: 'For Dad, for Dad.' He holds on even tighter, his fingers cramping up. The sea is angry and seems to have it in for the *Night Raider*.

Even more than she did before.

'How far do we have to go, Marvin?' he shouts up at the seagull.

'KRAA!' Marvin calls back, fighting against the wind.

They're nowhere near their destination yet, and Ravian knows that too.

A huge wave hits the deck. Some of the salty water crashes onto Ravian. He screams and hunches up his shoulders. His waterproof coat is no help against all that water. Against all that sea.

Then the sea starts heaving even more wildly. The *Night Raider* doesn't just roll to the left and right but pitches far forward and backward too, leaning at all kinds of strange angles. The wave that swept across the deck was only the beginning. Now all the waves are coming as high as the deck.

'Ravian!' shouts Kars. 'Are you holding on tightly?'

Ravian nods and puts up his thumb.

'Yes, and I can't fall off anyway!' he calls back, with a grin.

He hopes it'll hide how scared he is. It was such a wonderful moment this morning when he was standing at the rail with Kars, when he really thought he was getting less frightened. But maybe the sea noticed and now she's doing her best to change that. Ravian is an easy target.

Kars can't hear him any more. He's too busy tightening and knotting the ropes and making sure that the sail is positioned so that it won't rip or come loose in the wind. But the ropes keep coming untied and blowing in all directions.

'Marvin!' shouts Ravian. 'Please come down!'

Marvin gazes ahead and flies on with determination.

'Marvin, come on! We need to get through this storm first. The direction doesn't matter right now!'

And then Marvin does turn around. His wings drooping, he falls onto the deck and hides in a corner.

'Thank you,' Ravian says to him.

Marvin is just in time, because the wind is only getting stronger and wilder. A barrel blows over and rolls across the deck. The wind picks up a big net and tosses it into the sea. Bank stands firm at the wheel. He must have been through storms like this many times before, thinks Ravian. But keeping the ship upright is still a tough and tiring job.

And then everything that's not tied down is picked up by the wind and embraced by the sea: a bucket, the empty bottles, a big rope, two oil lamps, a box.

Ravian stoops to pick up Marvin, grabbing him under his wings. With slow, heavy steps, holding on tightly to the rail with his other hand, he carries Marvin below deck.

'Stay here, or you'll blow away!'

When Ravian turns around, the wind outside is so strong that he can hardly get through the door to the deck. Kars is still standing by the mast, fighting with the ropes. Ravian has to help him. There's no way Kars can do it alone!

'Kars!' Ravian shouts. Kars doesn't hear him. 'I'm coming!' Kars looks up briefly, but the rope slips from his hand again and the wind slaps it against his cheek. Like a really hard crack of a whip. Ravian sees it happen and he forces himself outside, back into the storm and through the rain. He has to get to Kars.

'Kars,' pants Ravian when he's close enough. 'You okay?'

'What?' shouts Kars. The wind howls, screaming in their ears.

Ravian points at his own cheek.

Kars frowns and then shakes his head.

'No, it's nothing. Here!' He hands Ravian one of the ropes. 'Hold tight!'

Ravian clasps both of his hands firmly around the rope. Scared of being whipped too, he concentrates really hard. But when he glances at Kars, he sees that the rope has sliced open Kars's cheek and dark-red blood is trickling down his face. Ravian tries to ignore his fear.

Hold on to the rope, he has to hold on to the rope. But he needs to hold on to himself too. He obviously can't leave the ship, but still he does whatever he can to avoid being blown away.

A powerful gust of wind knocks him in the back, as if two huge, bullying arms are giving him a shove.

Ravian falls against the mast, bumping his forehead on the wood. For a moment, he sees stars. But when he feels Kars's warm hand on his shoulder, he slowly comes round.

'You okay?' shouts Kars.

Ravian nods. His head is thumping a bit, but it doesn't really hurt. He'll have a bruise tomorrow, but it's not the worst that could happen.

'Here!' Kars yells into the wind. 'Hold on to that.' He points at a bit of railing that Ravian can just about reach.

'Shouldn't you be holding on too?' Ravian shouts back.

Kars shakes his head and stamps his left foot twice. 'Sea legs!'

Ravian takes hold of the rope again and turns away from Kars so that he can grab the railing. Just as his fingers close around it, another gust of wind blows up and a wave splashes out of from the angry sea and over Ravian. The wind seems to lift him into the air for a moment. He looks back at Kars. But Kars is no longer at his post.

The wind has picked Kars up and is holding him in the air. Like a piece of dandelion fluff, Kars is swirling on the wind. Higher and higher, and wilder and wilder.

'Kars!' Ravian screams at the top of his voice.

'Help!' Kars screams back. 'He's got me!'

Before Ravian can work out what to do, the wind throws Kars to the sea, so that she can catch him in her dark arms, like all the other things that blew away.

Kars smacks hard into the curse's invisible wall. It even seems to make a noise. He bounces straight back into the air, as if he landed on a trampoline. This time the wind doesn't catch him but abandons him to his fate. As Kars flies through the air, looking as if he's on his way to a hard landing on the deck, which would probably break every bone in his body . . . he gets caught in the net of the rigging.

Ravian's breath catches in his throat. Everything inside him·is screaming, and there are tears welling up in his eyes and waiting to fall. But there's nothing he can do. He's completely rigid, as if he's frozen. He looks at Kars, dangling there. His body, normally so strong, is limp, and he can't even hold up his head. Blood is dripping from his forehead. Is he unconscious? Or even . . .

'Kars!' Ravian hears the pirate shout. A huge flash of lightning splits the sky.

'You! Ravian!'

Bank's voice booms across the deck. 'Ravian, you have to take over at the wheel!'

'But I don't know how!' screams Ravian.

'You have to, lad!'

Ravian looks in panic at the pirate, then at Kars and back again. How is he supposed to sail this whole ship if he can't even hold on to one rope? But he has to. For Kars. With difficulty, he runs against the wind to the wheel.

'I have to save him!' screams Bank. 'If he falls from the rigging, it'll be the end of him!' He storms towards the mast.

Ravian has the enormous wheel in his hands. He thinks back to the steering lesson that Kars gave him the first day he was on board, when the pirate got so angry he sent them to scrub the hold. He must regret that now, because Ravian has no idea how to use the wheel. It's so incredibly hard to turn. It feels more like moving a boulder. Ravian tries again and hangs on one side with all his weight, trying to keep the ship upright.

'Bank!' Ravian shouts to the pirate, who turns to look at him. 'But what if *you* fall from the rigging?'

Bank stands still in the middle of all that natural violence, as if he's the eye of the storm.

'Then so be it! That boy's worth too much to me. I have to give it a try!'

And he walks onwards to the mast. He grabs a rope that he can get a good grip on. The pouring rain prevents Bank from looking straight up. The ship is still swaying violently from side to side, and the storm howls threateningly around the pirate.

Ravian holds his breath as he watches. Is Bank a brave sea hero? Does his crew really come first? Ravian doesn't care, just as long as Kars makes it. Oh, what will he do if it all goes wrong? There's a huge lump in his throat, and his back breaks out in a cold sweat. Don't think about that. It's going to be fine. At least they can't fall off the ship. For once, that's a comforting thought.

But it's hard not to be worried when he looks at Kars's helpless body dangling there in such danger.

Marvin sits inside, looking out through the window with a worried expression.

The pirate nimbly grasps the rigging and clamps his feet around the mast. But the wood is wet and slippery, and the wind taunts him, tugging at the ropes. His foot slips. His right hand lets go. He's hanging by his left arm now. With a huge roar, he takes hold of another rope with his right hand and pulls himself up. He plants his feet more firmly against the mast. One at a time, he moves his hands higher up the rope. Then he pulls and pushes himself up with his feet and his legs. With one last big shove, he reaches the place where Kars is hanging, like a fly caught in a spider's web.

Ravian can see that Bank is struggling. He has to hold on tightly with one hand while trying to untangle Kars with the other and then throw him over his shoulder too. The wind is protesting and doing his best to stop him. Then the sea sets another test for Bank: a whirlpool is swirling under and around the ship.

Ravian uses his full weight to try to keep the wheel under control. The pirate screams in exhaustion and anger, but then clamps his big legs around the mast in a kind of knot. By clenching his muscles tightly, he can just about manage to hold on to the mast. He reaches out his arms to Kars, who's still hanging there, unconscious. It takes all the pirate's strength, but he pulls Kars towards him. Puffing and panting, he screws up his whole face, which turns redder and redder. The wind furiously shakes the rigging. But Bank doesn't give up. He yanks the net towards him. Finally.

Now Kars is within reach and the pirate grabs hold of him. With the last of his strength, he throws Kars's limp body over his shoulders so that both of his hands are free, and he climbs back down.

Tears are streaming down Ravian's cheeks, and it's not just the wind. Is Bank holding on firmly enough to his friend?

Kars, please, stay here. Stay here. Stay with me, he silently pleads.

And then, just when Bank is almost back on the deck, his blistered leg loses its grip on the mast. Ravian freezes.

The pirate has nothing to hold on to. Kars and Bank fall the last part of the way to the deck. It must be almost twice Kars's height. A loud thud rings out, even through the commotion of the wind and the sea. In panic, Ravian lets go of the wheel.

Kars!

The moment they hit the deck, five purple flashes of lightning strike in a circle around the ship.

Ravian's never seen anything so terrifying and yet so beautiful.

There is complete silence, and the rain stops for a few seconds. As if the clouds are holding their breath.

What is the sea planning to do next?

But Ravian has no time to worry about her fury and her curse.

He has to get to Kars. If only he'd been standing there to catch him. To make sure his wounded body didn't have to suffer even more. How is he ever going to survive this?

Ravian runs towards them.

'Are you still alive? Bank! Kars!' he sobs.

Ravian doesn't hear anything. Only the vicious howling of the wind.

And then, finally, after seconds that seem to last for hours: 'Yes, blast it, stay at that wheel!'

16

THE ISLAND

In the boys' cabin, Kars is sleeping. Outside, the wind is still blowing wildly, but it seems to be slowly calming down.

Ravian has been sitting by Kars's bedside all night, taking care of his wounds, dabbing his brow and talking to him now and then. Sometimes Kars's breathing is heavy or he seems to be having a bad dream, but he hasn't woken up yet and so he hasn't replied to anything Ravian has said. Ravian's fearful thoughts and exhaustion are making it hard for him to come up with good stories, so he just talks about the adventures they've had together.

'Do you remember when we went oyster-catching, Kars? The way they were stuck to the rock? It was tricky, wasn't it? But we did get that beautiful pearl in return for all our hard work. And a delicious dinner, of course!'

Kars doesn't move, just breathes deeply.

'And do you remember when we found the secret room?' Ravian continues. 'When you get better, we'll try to open it again! I thought there might be a sea nymph in there! Or a whale! But, yeah, a whale wouldn't fit.' He chuckles awkwardly, not quite knowing what to do with himself and his feelings.

He rinses the cloth he's been using to dab Kars's forehead in the bucket of water beside him. Pirate Bank puts his head around the door. 'How's he doing?'

Ravian is amazed at the pirate's care and attention. He seems really upset that Kars has been hurt so badly. After that nasty fall, the two of them carried Kars to bed, cleaned his wounds and kept him warm. The pirate said there was nothing wrong with himself, but

Ravian could see that he was limping even worse than before. When the storm had died down, Bank got the ship back on course, with Marvin as his guide. But he keeps popping down to see how Kars is doing.

'Good,' he growls before limping back to his wheel.

'Bank's worried about you. Who'd have thought it?' Ravian whispers to Kars with a chuckle. 'In fact, he actually saved your life!'

Ravian gently wipes Kars's cheek with the wet cloth. The nasty bruise that the rope gave him has turned blue and purple, and the wound on his head is like a small volcanic crater. Ravian sings quietly, the way his dad always used to when Ravian couldn't sleep.

Sleep now, my laddie
and rest your sweet head
the fish in the sea
and you in your bed

Hush now, my laddie
my little sea dog
close your tired eyes
and sleep like a log

It sounds strange to hear it coming from another mouth than his dad's. He pauses for a moment to rinse the cloth in the water again. Then he dabs the beads of sweat from Kars's throat and continues with his song.

Find out, my laddie
what matters to you
set a good course
to your own self be true

But rest now, my laddie
and dream of the deep
the sea's waves will hold you
and rock you to sleep

Kars looks so fragile, lying there. Ravian hardly recognises him. He just wants to do the right thing. He wants him to wake up and recover. But Ravian knows that the longer he sleeps, the sooner the wound will heal.

'Kars . . .' he tries again, giving his arm a little squeeze. 'The storm's over.' Kars slowly opens his eyes.

Ravian smiles.

'Hey! You're awake!' A wave of relief washes through his body. All he really wants to do is to pick Kars up and hug him with joy. But he doesn't dare.

Kars groans.

'Don't worry, Kars. You're safe and you're going to get better. I'm right here. You've just got a bit of a cut on your head,' says Ravian as casually as possible. 'But that'll heal right up.'

Kars licks his dry lips.

'Do you want some water?' Ravian holds a cup up to him. Kars groans quietly, sits up and takes the cup. He has a few sips before lying back down.

'What happened?' he asks quietly.

'You blew away.'

'What?'

'And the curse actually saved you, but you still got hurt.' Ravian sighs. He suddenly feels very tired. He's so sad about everything's that's happened, and that Kars has ended up in such a bad state while Ravian himself is still in one piece.

'I'm so sorry, Kars.'

'What?'

'If we hadn't gone to look for my dad, we'd never have ended up in that storm. And you wouldn't have got hurt. It's my fault.'

Kars laughs carefully and gives Ravian's hand a squeeze. 'Yep, it's all your fault.'

Ravian snorts.

'Well, you know what I mean. I . . .'

'Don't be daft,' says Kars. And Ravian chuckles.

Then Marvin flies past the porthole and peeps in to see how Kars is doing.

Ravian waves at him.

'Look, there's Marvin. I think he wants to show us something. I'll just go up to the deck – if that's okay with you?'

Kars nods.

'Sleep a bit longer. It'll do you good. I'll make you some porridge.'

Kars smiles.

Ravian smiles back and heads outside.

'Well?' says Bank as soon as he sees Ravian walking across the deck.

'He's awake. I'm going to make some porridge for him.'

The pirate heaves a sigh of relief and turns his attention back to the wheel. Ravian heads to the galley, forgetting that he meant to go and see Marvin.

'GEP GEP GEP,' Marvin squawks at him from the rail. **'KLOW KLOW!'**

Smiling, Ravian walks over to him.

'Hey, Marv, what's up? Do you have some news?'

Marvin looks very happy, but Ravian doesn't understand why.

'Are we nearly there? Is that why you look so perky? But we won't be there for a long time, will we?' Marvin shakes his head. There's no sign of Lasse or land yet.

'**MEEEEW!**' Marvin squawks again. But Ravian shrugs and carries on to the galley. Sometimes it's annoying that he can't always understand Marvin. It'd be so nice if they could talk to each other. What would his voice sound like? Would all the words sound like squawks?

When Ravian returns to the deck, carrying the porridge for Kars, Marvin tries to get his attention again. He squawks and screeches and flies around Ravian's head, and then goes and sits on the rail. Then he drops off the rail and overboard. It looks as if he's fallen into the water, but he flies up again, just in time. He looks, hopefully and happily, at Ravian.

'Crazy bird,' says Ravian, walking back to their cabin.

Now that he feels a bit happier about Kars, Ravian can have a lie-down himself. And a rest. When he's given Kars his porridge, he falls asleep.

'Men!'

Ravian wakes with a start and sits up. What is it this time? A massive jellyfish? Is the sea angry again? He throws off the blankets and looks at Kars. He's lying on his back, asleep. His cheeks already have more colour, and he's looking better every day. Quietly, Ravian climbs out of bed and walks to the deck. The sun is high in the sky.

'Men!'

Bank's voice booms over the whole ship. They've been at sea for another five days since they were in that terrible storm – in the boxing ring with the sea and her henchman, the wind.

'Men, come and see!'

'What is it, Bank?' asks Ravian, rubbing his eyes. Then he sees Marvin, who greets him like a puppy.

'KLOW KLEEOW! GEP GEP KLOW!' he cries happily, landing on Ravian's head. He leans forward and looks at Ravian upside down.

'Hey, sunshine,' laughs Ravian, gently pushing Marvin upright and gazing into the distance. And there, on the horizon, he sees an island. An island with very tall trees.

He turns and looks at Bank, with surprise and hope on his face.

Bank is smiling.

'Yes, lad. I think that's where we're going.'

Ravian can't believe it.

'Is Dad there?' he shouts at Marvin. Marvin's eyes are gleaming like pearls.

Ravian goes to stand at the front of the ship to get a better look at their destination. As they approach the island, he sees beautiful white sand and tall trees with green leaves. Oh, land . . . It would be so wonderful to be able to walk with his bare feet in that soft, warm sand.

As they get even closer, Ravian spots something familiar: a beautiful old fishing boat with moss-green sails!

'Look! Look, Bank! That's my dad's boat!' shouts Ravian, pointing. 'That's where we need to go! That's where my dad is!'

He peers with narrowed eyes to see if he can spot Lasse.

'The boat must be damaged, eh, Marvin?'

Marvin nods.

Ravian is so eager to get there. He's never been so happy to see a boat before. But then he realises that he has no idea what to do when they get to the ship. They can't leave the *Night Raider*. So he can't go on land, and he can't give his dad a hug when he sees him, and they can't repair his dad's ship either. They can't do anything!

Kars's confused face suddenly appears in the doorway. He walks up to Ravian, squinting in the bright sunlight.

'Hey! What are you doing? Have you gone mad?' Ravian calls to him.

'Hi. Nope, don't think so,' Kars replies.

'Go back to bed, you idiot!' Ravian says sternly, but Kars is already standing almost beside him and looking in amazement at the island, which is getting closer and closer.

'So that's why you sounded so happy! We're there.'

Ravian nods and grins.

'And that's your dad's boat?'

'Yes! Moss-green sails. You can't miss it!'

Kars runs his hand through his hair and looks at Ravian with a big grin.

'Have you seen your dad yet? Or are we still too far away?'

Ravian shakes his head.

'No, I haven't seen him. Maybe he's inside the boat or he's gone for a walk or something.'

When the *Night Raider* is almost at the island and sailing very slowly through the shallow water by the beach, Ravian leans as far as he can over the rail.

'Be careful, won't you?' says Kars.

'What for? I can't fall anyway,' says Ravian. 'I can't get a proper look at the boat. So I don't know if my dad's there or what's wrong with the boat!'

Ravian leans even further forward. With his feet in the air, he balances with his waist on the rail. His fear seems to have completely vanished now. It's amazing what a cursed ship can do to a boy.

This is the moment Marvin's been waiting for.

At top speed, he flies hard into Ravian's dangling feet. Ravian loses his balance and doesn't manage to grab hold of the rail in time.

SPLASH!

He tumbles overboard. What on earth is happening?! Beneath the clear water, Ravian sees pink and purple plants and a big group of little yellow fish swimming past. A seahorse gallops right into Ravian's shoulder. And the shells on the bottom gleam and glitter more beautifully than gold. The sea can be so amazing! For a moment, it feels as if he's dreaming. He thought he'd never feel anything other than that ship under his feet ever again. And to be rocking *in* the waves rather than being tossed about in a ship *on* the waves is bliss. What a difference! But how is this possible? Has the curse been lifted? Has the sea forgiven them? Still underwater, he looks up at the sparkling sunlight and the blurry outline of the *Night Raider*.

Gasping for air, Ravian surfaces. Luckily, the water is shallow, so he can stand on the bottom. He's stunned. Marvin squawks away in delight.

Kars's eyes almost pop out of his head.

The pirate comes running and looks over the rail. Did that really just happen?

'What?!' shouts Bank. 'How did you get there? What are you doing? How did you manage that?'

Ravian can't speak. All he can do is laugh.

'But how?' the pirate repeats. He's so surprised that he seems almost angry. 'What about the curse? Where's the curse?'

He looks at Kars, who is leaning over the rail and joining in with Ravian's contagious laughter.

'Don't ask me! I don't have a clue!' he splutters.

'But . . . but . . .' stammers Bank. 'My ship! And . . . five days ago, you got bounced back by the curse. So, it was still in place then! And there's me, having all that trouble and worry for nothing. Oh, that sea! The salty devil does whatever she pleases, eh?'

Ravian grins at Kars. And then he looks at Bank. Good old Bank.

'I don't think,' says Kars, 'that it was all for nothing. I think maybe it was because you rescued me that the curse got lifted.'

The pirate frowns and wrinkles his bushy eyebrows.

'What does that have to do with it?'

Kars takes off his shirt and climbs over the rail.

'You were cursed for putting the lives of the former crew in danger by throwing them overboard, weren't you?' he says, climbing down the outside of the ship.

'Yes . . .'

'Well, this time you saved someone's life. Maybe that's why she's forgiven you!'

Bank's face relaxes and he tilts his head thoughtfully. Then he slowly nods.

'Of course! That must be it!' He roars with laughter, and Kars leaps into the water with a big grin. The water splashes into Ravian's face. When Kars comes up to the surface, they look at each other in disbelief. Then they start laughing again.

'Yes!' Ravian shouts from the water. 'The curse has been lifted!' He throws his arms into the air and then falls backwards and floats in the sea.

For the first time in his life, he puts himself in her hands.

17

LASSE

The squishy bottom of the sea, the wet sand with the hard shells, and the warm sand that sticks to his feet: it all feels wonderful. With every step, Ravian enjoys the sensation of his foot sinking a little into the sand. There's his dad's boat, tilted to one side on the sand. Is Lasse inside? Maybe working on the repairs? As Ravian comes closer, he sees that there are quite a few holes in the bottom. What's happened?

He clutches his dad's ring. Now that he's so close to finding him, he misses him all the more. Marvin flies after Ravian and sits on the edge of the boat.

'Dad?' Ravian walks all the way around it, but the boat appears to be deserted. He'd expected to find some traces: clothes, food, tools. Ravian climbs on board. There are a few familiar things: his dad's big book about seafarers, a small wooden box with a cat on it, and a big green shirt, almost the same colour as the sails. Ravian picks up the shirt and smells it. Strange how your dad's old sweat doesn't smell that bad.

'Hey!'

Ravian turns around. It's Bank, staggering towards him across the loose sand.

'Hey!' Ravian shouts cheerfully. 'Have you come to help me?'

'Help you? I just wanted to feel that sand! Fantastic! By all the Seven Seas! Oh, oh! I haven't felt anything like this for ten years!'

Bank puts his hands in the air and jumps up and down. His long, greasy locks dance around.

Ravian chuckles. Bank wriggles his toes in the soft sand and then looks thoughtfully at Lasse's boat. It's much smaller than the *Night Raider*, of course, but it has a lot more nets. It's a real fishing boat, with a small cabin and just a few portholes. It's a simple vessel, not the grand, regal ship that Bank is used to.

'Have you found him yet?'

Ravian shakes his head.

'Well, that's great. You've found his ship, but he's still lost without a trace!'

'Where's Kars?'

'Sent him back to bed. He'll come later.'

Pirate Bank falls backwards onto the sand. He moves his arms and legs to make a sand angel – a ridiculously large one. Then he gets up and runs back to the sea. He sinks to his knees in the surf.

'Thank you, almighty sea. My eternal thanks,' Ravian hears him saying. As soon as he has spoken those words, a huge wave washes over him, which he welcomes with open arms. The wave swirls around the pirate a few times. Bank closes his eyes and breathes a deep sigh of relief.

Their battle is over, thinks Ravian. Finally the pirate and the sea have stopped fighting.

Then Ravian sees a woman, walking barefoot past Bank and towards him. Her sweet face is framed by very long orange-brown hair, which ripples behind her in waves, and she's wearing an almost see-through pale-pink gown, which makes Bank gulp. Could this be the woman Ravian imagined Lasse falling in love with?

From far away among the trees, there's the sound of a loud drum. And music. Voices singing. Is that where his dad is? His dad does like a party, after all.

'Bank! Shall we go and take a look?' shouts Ravian.

He climbs down off the damaged boat, and Marvin flies to his favourite spot on Ravian's shoulder.

'Hello, miss,' Ravian says politely to the woman who is just walking by. She looks like a goddess, even though Ravian doesn't really know what goddesses look like.

'Um . . . hello,' she says awkwardly. She doesn't seem quite so much like a goddess now.

'Is there a party over there?' He points at the trees.

She shrugs and pulls a face.

'Don't know,' she says. 'Must be those crazy people again.' She rolls her eyes and shakes her head. As she walks away, Ravian hears her muttering, 'Great, more flotsam washed up on the island.'

With a frown on his face, Ravian watches her go. Then he waves Bank over. The pirate watches the woman, open-mouthed, for just a little too long, but then stands up. Ravian sighs and laughs. Why was Bank staring at the woman like that? It's a mystery to him.

Bank quietly follows Ravian, who is already exploring. The bark of the trees is nice and smooth. The ground is sandy, but there are a lot of twigs. And there are low bushes everywhere with leaves that are so big and green that they look fake. When Ravian gazes upward, he sees big red fruits hanging in the trees. What a wonderful island. Dad could have done a lot worse.

'Is Kars going to be okay by himself?' he asks.

The pirate nods.

'Yes, lad. He needs to rest.'

They walk through the trees towards the sound of the party.

'Well, we need to do something, don't we?' someone shouts. Bank, Marvin and Ravian are so close that they can clearly make out what's being said now.

'I'll tell you one thing,' another voice says. 'We're not letting him go. No way!'

Ravian wonders what's going on.

And then he hears a very familiar voice: 'Please, gentlemen, please! I have to ... I need to leave this place!'

Lasse!

'Dad!' shouts Ravian. But the pirate puts his hand over Ravian's mouth.

'Shush, you nitwit! You don't know what kind of people they are, do you?'

'I don't care!' Ravian struggles out of the pirate's grasp. 'And I have you, don't I? You were going to help me.'

The pirate gives no reply and doesn't move as Ravian runs towards the voices. Marvin flies along with him. Ravian has never been so happy. He doesn't even feel the branches hitting him and the thorns scratching him.

'Dad! Can you hear me?'

The voices fall silent. Ravian stops running. He stands still and shivers. It's not happening again, is it? He just heard his dad – but was it *really* him?

'Ravian?'

'Dad!'

'Ravian!'

He pushes the leaves aside and finds himself in a clearing. And there, gleaming in the warm sunlight, he sees his dad's blond curls. And his blue eyes and his kind face. Lasse bursts out laughing with surprise and relief, and a tear trickles down his face when he sees his son standing there. Ravian's breath catches in his throat. It seems like a beautiful dream. Or a nightmare – because then he sees that Lasse is tied to a tree.

'Dad, what are they doing?' he cries out in panic. 'Why are you tied up?'

'Ravian, calm down . . .' Lasse says soothingly.

'Why have you tied up my dad?' yells Ravian.

He takes a good look at the men who are surrounding Lasse. One has a big moustache and he's wearing a red coat with gold buttons, but it's all torn and stained. The other men's clothes are just as filthy: grubby white shirts, ripped trousers, boots with the soles hanging loose. And bead necklaces with fruits on. They're all very thin, with sunken cheeks. They have strange expressions on their faces, and their eyelids keep twitching. One of them is jerking and looking around, as if there's a fly buzzing about his head. Which there probably is, with that stink. Another is jabbing a stick into Lasse's side and seems completely unaware of what's going on around him.

'Ah . . . and who might this be?' The man in the red coat comes threateningly towards Ravian.

'I'm Ravian. And get your hands off my dad! I'm here to rescue him!' He tries to make himself look as big as possible.

Perched on Ravian's shoulder, Marvin glares at the man, who just bursts out laughing.

The man bursts out laughing.

'Okay. You and this bird, eh?'

Ravian nods.

'Well, isn't that good news?' hisses the man. 'Because seagulls are our favourite treat!' He laughs out loud, and the rest of the men laugh along with him this time. He takes a step forward and makes a chomping sound with his teeth, right next to Marvin.

Ravian tries not to show that he's scared, but Marvin pecks the man right on the nose.

'Ow! Blasted creature!' grumbles the man, taking a step back.

Ravian chuckles and bravely walks towards his dad.

'Hey, you can't just do that!' says one of the gang, blocking the way. He takes a rope out of his back pocket. With an unexpectedly strong grip, he ties Ravian's hands behind his back.

'Ow!' shouts Ravian, trying to wriggle free. Marvin flies at the man and pecks and scratches his face.

The man angrily throws Ravian down next to Lasse.

'No, keep your hands off him!' shouts Lasse, but the man doesn't listen.

Ravian struggles to his feet. There's sand on his face, and his knees are burning. He glares at the man. Then he goes to stand beside Lasse and puts his head on his dad's chest. 'Hey, son,' says Lasse, 'and lovely Marvin, I'm so glad to see you both. You did so well, Marvin, taking my ring to my son. And bringing my son to me!'

He lovingly rests his own head against his son's.

Ravian feels tears of happiness welling up but swallows them away. He has to stay focused now, or he'll never be able to escape and defeat these men. First trapped on a ship, and now on a strange island. Is there no end to his troubles?

'However did you find your way here?' asks Lasse.

'Well, I just . . . left home. You were gone and I was worried, and then . . . then I went on a ship, with a pirate, and . . .' Ravian looks around. Where has Bank got to?

He looks at the bushes and spots Bank's old handkerchief and a few tufts of his dirty hair in among the leaves. And then his eyes, peering out. When Bank sees Ravian looking at him, he puts a finger to his lips. Is he hiding? Is he scared? But that gigantic pirate should be able to handle these scrawny little men, shouldn't he?

'You? On a ship?' says Lasse. 'With a pirate?'

'Yes, but he's actually pretty nice,' says Ravian, 'and you're here with a bunch of pirates too, aren't you?' He turns away from Bank and looks around the group with raised eyebrows. 'I think I should be more worried about you than you are about me!'

Lasse laughs out loud.

'You've grown so big,' he says quietly.

'Hang on, just one second . . .' says one of the men. He's dressed in a pair of trousers with a blue-and-white striped blanket tied around his shoulders like a sort of cape. Around his neck, there's a big rusty key. 'We are not pirates!'

'Well, that's what you look like,' says Ravian. 'Like a bunch of wild ruffians!'

'You've got some nerve!' shouts the man in red. 'Is it just because I've got a parrot on my shoulder?'

'You don't have a parrot on your shoulder,' says Ravian, pointing.

The man looks in confusion at his shoulder and blinks a few times.

'Ah . . . yes. That's right. I lost it,' he says. 'But anyway, we're not pirates! We did use to be seafarers, very successful ones, with a beautiful ship. But, um . . . I lost that too.' The man fiddles nervously with one of the buttons on his coat. Ravian rolls his eyes and looks at his dad with a question on his face. Who *are* these people?

'Hey! Stop that!' shouts one of the men. Marvin is pecking the rope around Ravian's hands and trying to undo it. There's a lot of flapping and squawking involved.

The man claps his hands in front of Marvin's face to chase him away, but Marvin ignores him. So the man grabs Marvin by one leg and throws him into a big saucepan and puts the lid on. Then he sits on it.

'No! Marvin!' Ravian shouts, panicking. 'Stop that! You can't just take everyone prisoner for no reason!'

'Oh yes, we can,' taunts the man in red.

'Why us? Why my dad? Why me and my friend now too? Let him go!' Ravian has never felt his head boiling like this before. How dare they?!

'Well, laddie, you wouldn't know about this, but your father is the answer to the riddle of the sea.'

'Huh?' Pirate Bank's growling voice comes from the bushes. A branch cracks. Not everyone hears him, but the man who's standing closest turns around. Bank ducks down, just in time.

'And you and your bird friend should mind your own business.'

'What do you mean by "the answer to the riddle"?' Ravian asks.

The man clears his throat and begins: 'Leaf in the wind, top bright with sun, haul it in, guard it well . . .'

'And wait till you've won,' Ravian says, interrupting him.

The man in red raises an eyebrow.

'Aha, so you *do* know the riddle!'

Lasse looks at Ravian in surprise. 'You know it?' he whispers.

Ravian gives his dad a quick nod.

'Yes, I'll tell you about it later,' he whispers. Still furious, he turns back to the man. 'But Lasse isn't a leaf in the wind!'

'Well, laddie, think about it: his ship came sailing here like a leaf in the wind, with its green sails and the storm blowing it along.'

Ravian looks questioningly at Lasse.

'And his hair is gold like the sun. We spotted that straight away. Like a bit of sunshine on his head. And on his head – that's on top.'

Ravian nods. It's farfetched, but there could be something to it.

'So then we knew that we had to haul your father in and not let him go. To guard him well. And then wait till we've won. So, we'll obviously need to keep him. It's very nice of you to come to rescue him, but he's not going anywhere. But, um . . . we still don't really know exactly what that last part's about. We're still waiting, to tell the truth.'

'The ship!'

It just pops out of Bank's mouth, who's still well hidden.

The man who's standing close to Bank looks back again and now he sees his face among the green leaves.

'Hey . . . wait a second . . . Th-that's . . .' he stammers quietly. He stoops to take a closer look. 'It is! It's him! It's Pirate Bank! And he's getting away!'

18

THE CREW

Pirate Bank runs through the water and climbs back aboard the *Night Raider*.

Kars is sitting on a box in the shade, and he looks at him in astonishment.

'Back already?' he says calmly.

Bank looks panicky and he's panting.

'The . . . They . . .' He points at the beach.

Kars stands up to see what he's pointing at. A man comes running after the pirate. And then more appear from the trees.

'Who are they?'

Bank doesn't reply but grabs the last bottle, which is on the deck. He doesn't look at Kars until he's taken three big swigs.

'They're . . . um . . . old acquaintances,' he says.

There's a big group of men standing on the beach now.

'They've all got these funny looks on their faces,' says Kars.

'They do? What like?' the pirate asks nervously.

'Well, um . . . kind of amazed. Like they've seen an angel or something.'

The man in the red coat wades with open arms to the ship and stands right up against it, with his arms spread wide. As if he wants to give it a big hug.

'Oh, oh, my love! My beloved! *This* was it. This is the answer to the riddle. Finally!' he cries. 'This is why we needed Lasse. Us keeping him captive is what brought our beloved *Night Raider* back to us. Oh, the sea has her weird and wonderful ways!' He bends to kiss the water rippling around his feet.

'Um . . . Bank? That man's hugging our ship . . .' says Kars, his eyebrows raised. 'And kissing the sea.'

'Excuse me?! *Your* ship?' the man shouts. 'This ship is *ours*!'

Kars looks at the pirate with a mixture of surprise and suspicion on his face.

'Bank! Blast it! Give me back my ship!'

Bank leans over the rail and looks down.

'Erm . . . nope,' he says, in a teasing voice, but he's clearly deadly serious.

'How dare you come here? On my ship? Well, I'm not going to let you sail away with it on my watch. Not again!' the man in the red coat shouts furiously.

'Bank!' says Kars, deciding to get involved now. 'Is this . . . the crew?'

'We most certainly are,' says the man in the blanket cape, who is now wading through the waves as well. 'This is Captain Caius.' He points at the man in the red coat. 'And I'm Jur, his first mate. Nice to meet you!' he says solemnly. 'Right, come on, captain. Let's go on board and take her back!'

'Hang on a moment. Why don't we try solving this with words first?' says Captain Caius. It seems he can remember only too well how it went last time.

Kars looks at Bank.

'But, um . . .' he asks quietly, 'weren't they all supposed to be dead?'

'I thought so too!' shouts Bank. 'Holy mackerel! I couldn't believe my eyes when I saw them standing there. Yes, and now they want her back, of course. My beautiful ship. But I can't just –'

'Where's Ravian?' Kars says, interrupting him.

Bank waves his hand towards the trees on the island.

'Over there. With his dad, who's tied up.'

'He's found Lasse?' asks Kars with a happy grin. And then, worried: 'Tied up? And what about Ravian?'

'Yes, yes. Him too. And Marvin. But, um, it'll be fine.'

Kars has a lump in his throat. He looks at the pirate through narrowed eyes and then shakes his head. What kind of terrible mess has he got Ravian into now? Kars is going to have to sort this out. He turns to Captain Caius and coughs gently.

'Excuse me, sir, um, captain, why are you holding Lasse prisoner?' he asks politely. His voice cracks when he thinks about the others. 'And Ravian and Marvin?'

'We had to. The riddle said so. Yes, he's the answer all right. I never really understood why, but now I do,' says Captain Caius. 'He and his boat washed ashore on the beach. There were holes in the boat, which had been damaged in a storm. When he came to ask us for help, we knew exactly what to do. Haul him in, guard him well.' He nudges his first mate Jur and whispers something in his ear. Jur smiles.

'This, um . . . Lasse, eh . . . He must be worth a lot to you, right?' he says slyly.

'Yes, captain!' Kars says quickly. 'He's our friend's dad. And we've been looking for him for a long time. Ravian's worth at least as much to us too.'

Pirate Bank gives Kars a prod in the side.

'You nitwit,' he says quietly.

'Ah yes, I'd noticed that,' says the captain. 'Well, in that case, I have an idea.'

Kars rubs his side, glaring at Bank.

'What if you give us back that ship,' the captain continues, 'and then we'll give Lasse back to you? And the little guy and that feathery fellow too.' He throws his hands in the air to emphasise what a generous gesture this is.

'No,' says Bank immediately.

'Hey, Bank! What are you doing? We want to get them freed, don't we?' hisses Kars.

'No. *You* want to get them freed. I want to keep my ship. Especially now that I'm rid of that curse. So, I can go adventuring, stealing treasure and winning hearts!'

'Ah, good luck with that, you old goat,' Jur calls from the water.

Bank glares at him.

'Yes, but, Bank, if we . . .' whispers Kars, putting his hand in front of his mouth so that the others can't hear him.

'An excellent plan!' Bank's eyes gleam.

'Okay, this is our offer,' says Kars in a business-like voice. 'We'll give you the ship.'

The men let out deafening cheers.

'On condition that . . .' Kars says, interrupting them. 'On condition that you release Ravian, Marvin and Lasse – *and* give us whatever's inside that secret room!'

The men gasp.

Jur reaches to clutch the key around his neck.

'Oh, n-no . . .' he stammers.

Bank and Kars give each other nods of satisfaction.

'Yes, I saw you with that key,' Kars says, pointing at it. 'There's only one thing it could be for.'

'But no . . . that's . . . you can't . . . Captain?' Jur stammers quietly.

Captain Caius bows his head. He holds his hand up to the trembling Jur.

'No, Jur, just calm down.' He lays his hand on the side of the *Night Raider*. 'We're home now.'

Jur's jaw drops. 'What? But the tr—'

'We agree!' shouts Captain Caius. 'Men, release the gentlemen and the bird and bring them here. Tonight, we will drink to this day. As friends.' He gives Bank a grumpy look and then a cautious smile. 'All of us.'

When Jur and Captain Caius have climbed aboard, Kars and Bank follow them curiously to the hold, where Bank pushes aside all the crates in front of the door to the secret room. Jur takes the key from around his neck and slides it into the lock. The door swings open.

'Barnacles and bilgewater!' says the pirate, his eyes shining like a magpie's. 'I'd never have dared to dream of this!'

19

PARTY

'See what you've done, captain? Had you forgotten about it?' Jur bursts into tears when he sees the secret room. But Captain Caius shakes his head.

'Jur, don't you think this ship, this beautiful ship, is worth much more than that?' Jur looks sheepish. 'This is the ship given to me by my father, who had it from his father, and he got it from his father. This ship is all that makes us mean something, Jur. Do you understand that? It doesn't feel like something I own. I *am* this ship. It's my soul. And my soul was taken from me by this idiot!' roars Captain Caius.

'Kars! Kars! Do you see this?' Pirate Bank has never bellowed so loud before. With his enormous boots, he stomps into the room. In the middle sit ten big chests bursting with pearls.

Great big gleaming pearls.

Kars nods in amazement. Just that one pearl was amazing, but this? Wow!

Bank puts his hands in one of the chests. They disappear into the treasure. When he takes them back out, pearls are slowly running through his fingers.

'Oh, Kars! So this has been sailing along with us all this time!' he marvels. 'Such good fortune! What a joy!'

Captain Caius's face clouds over a little as he sees Bank playing with his precious treasure.

'Can I have my ship back now?' he asks.

Bank doesn't react.

'Hey, you old dog!' shouts Captain Caius. Jur is standing in a corner, looking with big eyes at the pearls. At the same time, he's keeping close watch on

Bank and Kars. Then he takes a handful of pearls and carefully slips them into his pocket. But Bank notices immediately. Furiously, he stares at Jur.

'You sneaky little weasel!' With one big pirate's step, he's standing with his nose in Jur's face. 'You want the same treatment as last time, do you?'

Jur gulps.

Captain Caius lays his hand on Bank's shoulder.

'It's my ship,' he says.

Grumpily, Bank turns to look at him.

'Where are Lasse, Ravian and Marvin, then?' Kars asks quickly.

The captain puts his hand to his ear and points up.

'I think I hear them coming!'

Out on the deck, all the men are still admiring their ship. Marvin watches from the mast with sparkling eyes.

Lasse and Ravian climb aboard.

'See, this is where I was trapped for so long,' says Ravian. He sounds so cheerful that it's almost as if he enjoyed it. 'This is where I was trapped by the curse!'

Lasse nods, looking a little worried. 'But you're quite happy wandering around a ship these days? I can't believe my eyes, son!'

Ravian gives him a big, proud grin. Then he sees Bank, Kars, Caius and Jur coming out of the hold.

'Look, Dad,' he whispers, pulling Lasse's hand. '*That's* Kars!'

When they're all on deck, Ravian runs over to Kars and throws his arms around him. After a long hug, he peers anxiously at the bandage that's still on Kars's head.

'How is it?'

'Good, and getting better and better,' replies Kars. Then he spots the big blond man who's beaming at them.

'You must be Lasse,' Kars says happily, striding towards him.

'And you're Kars! It's so good to meet you.' And they throw their arms around each other, as if they've known each other for years.

'I've heard a lot about you,' Lasse says to Kars. With a wink, he adds in a whisper, 'In what was actually a very short time.'

'Really?' Kars says with a doubtful grin. 'I certainly *have* heard a lot about *you*, though! This one here just kept telling story after story!' He points over his shoulder at Ravian. Lasse laughs.

'Ravian!' shouts the pirate. 'Lad, you have to come and take a look down here! Come on. Come and see what I've found.'

'Um . . . Bank? Why don't you take a look at what *I've* found first?' says Ravian, pointing at his dad.

Lasse walks up to the pirate.

'So, Mr Pirate, you've been taking good care of my son, have you?'

'Yes, um . . . Call me Bank. That's my name. And, um, taking care of, hmm, well . . .' the pirate says. He looks sheepishly at Ravian, rubbing his blistered leg, which has almost healed. 'More like him taking care of me, I think.'

Lasse and Ravian give each other a grin.

'Yes, I always have the same feeling,' replies Lasse, shaking the pirate by the hand. 'But thank you anyway. Thank you for bringing him to me and thanks for freeing me.'

Bank answers Lasse with a wary nod.

Marvin has come to sit on Ravian's shoulder, in his old familiar spot.

'Come on,' says Bank again. 'You coming, too?' he asks Lasse. The five of them walk to the hold.

'Blimey!' exclaims Ravian when he sees what's gleaming behind the door. He picks up a pearl and takes a closer look.

'This is all mine now!' the pirate shouts happily, picking up a handful of pearls and sprinkling them over himself. Kars looks at him with raised eyebrows.

'Ours, I mean,' mumbles Bank.

'How did that happen?' asks Ravian.

'In exchange for the ship.'

'But I thought you already traded my dad for the ship? That's what those men said when they untied us.'

'Yes, that too. But this is a bonus,' says the pirate. 'I didn't think it was enough otherwise. Nothing personal, mind.' He puts his thumb up at Lasse, who's also gawping at the pearls.

'This is amazing!' says Ravian. 'Now I have everyone here with me, and we're rich too!'

Lasse runs his hand through Ravian's curls.

'But how are we going to take all this home?' asks Ravian. Suddenly he realises that getting back to Rottenherring isn't going to be easy. Lasse's ship is damaged, they've lost the *Night Raider*, and no one has a clue where exactly they are.

'Dad?' he says quietly. 'How are we going to get home? Oh, and Kars is coming with us too, by the way!'

Kars gives Ravian's hand a grateful squeeze.

'Of course Kars can come. And Bank as well, if he likes,' says Lasse. 'We'll just have to smile nicely at the crew and ask if they'll drop us off at home. But I don't think everyone's going to like that idea.' The pirate shakes his head. There's no way he'll sail on his own ship with someone else as the captain, Ravian guesses. Not a chance!

'Then we'll just have to work together to repair my boat.'

'What's the problem?' asks Bank.

'Some holes were knocked in the side when I hit the rocks in a bad storm. We'll need to seal them up, but the biggest problem will be making them waterproof. We'll have to get our hands on caulking cotton, and tar and wood.'

Bank starts searching and rummaging around in the hold. He opens a chest and looks inside a cupboard.

'It'll be done in a jiffy. I've got everything you need! We can do it all tomorrow.'

Lasse smiles with relief, but Ravian frowns doubtfully.

'That belongs to the crew now, doesn't it?' he asks.

'Oh . . . yes,' sighs Bank.

'But isn't it part of setting Lasse free?' says Kars. 'I'll go and talk to the men.'

Less than a minute later, he's back.

'I've sorted it out!'

'Good,' says Lasse, giving Kars a grateful smile. 'It's not complicated. I'd have been able to get it done pretty quickly if that bunch of madmen hadn't captured me,' he says to Ravian. 'I wanted to head for home two months ago!'

'Everything is going to be fine,' says Bank. 'The repairs won't take long. But first we're going to have a big party on the beach!'

Ravian could give the pirate a hug. He can hardly believe he ever thought he was frightening.

It's a huge celebration. The men have built a big campfire. They've collected all the rum they could find, and they're all drinking plenty of it. The crew are dancing wildly around the fire, kicking one leg very high in the air, then turning around and doing the same with the other leg. One of the men is playing the drum, and some are singing at the top of their voices. Jur is the first to finish a whole bottle and he dances the most wildly of all. Then Ravian spots the woman with the long hair again, sitting a short distance away in a big shell by a tree, and he sees Jur running over to her.

Ravian is sitting peacefully on the sand, between Kars and his dad. And Marvin is sitting in front of him, a little closer to the fire. Without his friend Marvin, none of this would have happened. Ravian stares into the flames, as he often does at home in Rottenherring, because it calms him down. But now he really does feel calm. He breathes a sigh of happiness.

Pirate Bank drops down beside them. Lasse nods at him, as he would at a friend. They're both holding bottles of rum, which they raise to each other.

'So,' the pirate says, 'it's back to Rottenherring, is it?'

Ravian nods. 'You remembered the name.'

'Will you come with us, Bank?' asks Lasse.

Ravian smiles. 'Why would Bank want to go there, Dad?'

Lasse looks expectantly at Bank. He seems to know something . . .

'Well? Why *would* you want to go there?'

Bank shyly lowers his eyes.

'Well . . . I have, um . . . Someone's waiting for me,' he splutters.

Ravian looks at him in surprise, and Lasse gives a satisfied chuckle.

'Someone's waiting for you? In Rottenherring?' asks Ravian.

Bank nods. He seems to be blushing, although it's hard to tell in the dim light. He gulps.

'Elin's waiting for me.'

'Elin? I don't know anyone called Elin in Rottenherring. That's odd. I thought I knew everyone . . . Dad, do you know an Elin?'

Lasse smiles.

'You certainly do know her,' he says. 'She lives in that house along the secret path to the harbour.'

'The Weeping Woman?!' Ravian exclaims.

Then he turns to the pirate. 'She's waiting for *you*?'

Bank looks shocked.

'You call her the Weeping Woman?' he asks, his voice trembling. 'But she's always so happy!'

'Not any more,' says Ravian, shaking his head. 'No. She cries almost all the time. Which is why we call her that, of course.'

Pirate Bank looks as if he's about to start crying too.

He actually looks just like Elin.

'Hey, Bank,' says Lasse, 'she told me all about it. There's no need to worry. She understood that you had to go away, to go to sea. She's lived in the harbour all her life, and she knows how it is with sailors. It's just that she was heartbroken when she heard about the curse. No one could cheer her up. She loved you. Truly. And I think she still does.'

Bank nods and stares at the waves breaking in the surf.

'Come with us, and we'll go to see her together.'

'Yes, and you can take one of those big pearls for her. That's sure to make her feel better,' suggests Kars. He looks at Ravian and gives him a quick wink.

'Yes, or why not make it a whole crate?' cries Ravian.

Bank smiles. 'No, lads, it doesn't work like that. It's not that easy.'

'But she *will* be happy to see you again,' says Lasse. 'At least think about it.'

After two days on the island, they're ready to leave. 'There!' shouts Lasse, nailing the last plank to the boat. 'That's it!'

Kars flaps the front of his shirt. All that hard work has made him hot. Ravian is wearing Lasse's old handkerchief on his head again. Bank is standing by the crates of pearls, which are on the beach, waiting to be loaded onto the boat. He'd rather not admit it, but he felt a bit tearful yesterday when the *Night Raider* sailed away with her old crew.

So, Ravian and Bank can load the crates now. When Ravian picks one up, it's actually pretty easy.

'Hey, that's strange . . .' he says. 'This crate is so light!'

No one seems to hear him. Are pearls not that heavy, or has he got a lot stronger . . . ?

'Will you hoist the sails, Bank?' asks Lasse when they're ready to go. One by one, they climb aboard.

Bank tugs on the ropes and, with a loud clattering, the wind fills the moss-green sails.

'Right, boys,' says Lasse in a dreamy voice, 'we're finally sailing for home!'

'KLOW! KLOW!' Marvin cries, flying around the mast.

'Dad?'

'Yes, Rav?'

'How long does a seagull live?'

Lasse looks at the happily circling Marvin.

'About twenty-five years. But there was once a seagull that made it to almost fifty!'

'Ha, that's old,' says Kars, coming to stand beside Ravian and putting his arm around his shoulders.

Ravian nods and waves up at his flying friend. 'We're going to have so much fun!'

Thank you for choosing a Piccadilly Press book.

If you would like to know more about our authors, our books or if you'd just like to know what we're up to, you can find us online.

www.piccadillypress.co.uk

And you can also find us on:

We hope to see you soon!